As the older officer walked around the squad car to get in on the driver's side, the young one turned to Earl, who was sitting in the backseat. "You lowlife bastard," he said, "you. . . ." He didn't get a chance to complete his statement. Earl hit him between the eyes, and before the young officer could retaliate, he hit him again.

He was a black streak, throwing punches from the shoulder. The officer managed to open the door, but as he staggered out, Earl jumped from the backseat and buffeted him with a barrage of punches until the officer slumped to the curb. A warning was sounded from the crowd, but before Earl could spin around, the older officer hit him from behind with his blackjack, and Earl slipped quietly to the sidewalk.

Holloway House Classics by Donald Goines

Dopefiend

Whoreson

Crime Partners

Death List

Kenyatta's Last Hit

Black Gangster

Black Girl Lost

STREET PLAYERS

DONALD GOINES

Kensington Publishing Corp.
www.kensingtonbooks.com

HOLLOWAY HOUSE CLASSICS are published by

Kensington Publishing Corp.
119 West 40th Street
New York, NY 10018

ISBN-13: 978-0-7582-9463-0
ISBN-10: 0-7582-9463-8
First Kensington Trade Paperback Printing: July 2014

10 9 8 7 6 5 4 3 2

Printed in the United States of America

STREET PLAYERS

1

EARL'S APARTMENT WAS elaborately, tastefully, and expensively furnished. The three young men lounging on the floor had completely disregarded the plush gold velvet couch and matching chairs to stretch out on the deep-pile, red wall-to-wall carpet. Charles, a tall Negro with brown, bumpy skin and a high natural, began crawling towards the coffee table while Earl and the others watched listlessly. "Anybody want me to roll them a joint?" he asked.

"You can twist me another, as long as you're at it, man," Billy, a slim, dark-complexioned black man called from the far corner. Billy pushed the cushion from beneath his head and rose to a sitting position, patting his hair lightly, pushing the process back in place. He eyed Earl, who was standing across the room looking out of the picture window. "Say, Earl," he said, "let's call up some square bitches and have them come over and dig this penthouse of yours, man."

Earl, tall and brown-skinned, ran his fingers across his mustache, smiled, and walked to the glass-topped coffee table where Charles was busy twisting reefers. He picked up a joint and pointed it towards Billy before lighting up. "That's the reason I *got* this penthouse, Billy, instead of some run-down, cold-water flat across town," he said.

"What the hell you mean by that?" Duke, the fourth member of the group, asked as he came over and joined the men at the table. He accepted one of the joints Charles held out to him.

Earl took a slow drag from his reefer before answering. "I'd feel like a damn fool if we had some square bitches sitting around getting high and one of my whores should happen to come home," he said.

Billy picked up a cushion and tossed it over beside the table so that he could kneel on it. "What difference would it make? You're supposed to be the one doing the pimping, Earl, not one of your whores."

Duke laughed loudly. "I ain't got nothing to do with it, Earl, but Billy is pulling your coat to the real."

"Pimping is my livelihood, nigger, so I don't need any goddamn instructions!" Earl replied sarcastically. "Neither you nor Billy would give me a goddamn penny towards my rent or car note if I blew my whores, so don't worry about how I take care of *my* business."

"Goddamn, baby," Billy replied jokingly. "If someone who didn't know us heard you talking, they wouldn't believe we was real cool with each other."

"That's right," Duke yelled, putting his two cents in. He removed a large bankroll and began counting hundred-dollar bills on the table. "I'll gladly loan you any parts of this case, if you need it, man. Go ahead, take what you want."

Charles twisted up the last reefer. "Why don't you motherfuckers quit bullshittin'. If it wasn't for them bitches Earl got out on the track, he couldn't borrow five dollars, let alone some big stuff. That ain't nothing but neck—and the side of it at that— that you're talkin' out of!"

Earl spoke up with the youthful gaiety and irresponsibility of a young man who didn't care what others thought of him. "Ain't nobody asked your greasy black ass to loan me no money, so you can quit flashing that little roll of yours. You sure in the hell ain't impressing nobody with that A-D-C trap money."

Duke stuffed his bankroll back into his pocket. "Okay, nigger, I hear you rappin'. Just 'cause you got this pad up here, you must think that makes you one hell of a pimp."

Earl laughed harshly. "They rent these penthouses to anybody, Duke. All you got to do is be handling."

All of the men laughed, while Duke sneered, revealing a perfect set of evenly spaced, well-kept teeth. There was a constant undercurrent of competitiveness between the men in the apartment. None really trusted the other, not where their women were concerned. It was great sport for one to end up by taking one of his friends' girls.

Duke continued his harassment. "I still don't know how you went about getting this place, Earl. You sure don't look like no peckerwood. What did you do, send one of your white girls up to rent it?"

Again the men in the room laughed. Earl adjusted his pants and straightened his shirt. "Whatever I did, Duke, you can bet I did it like a player. In fact, if you should want a place here and can't get it because of your extremely dark man-tan, you can let your white girl rent it, and you put on a white jacket and carry her bags in for her."

"That ain't nothing but bullshit ya keep kickin' back and forth," Billy said suddenly. "I don't understand it, but every time you two get together, it always ends with both of you trying to drop lugs on each other."

Charles nodded in agreement. "That's right. Instead of pimps, you act like two bitches."

Earl and Duke glared at the other two men. Neither man actually wanted to discontinue the light exchange. Both men had a hidden dislike for one another, and yet they ran together almost every day.

"Let's ride down on the whores and see who's

catching them the biggest," Duke said suddenly as he stood up.

A dry, bitter laugh escaped from Earl. "Since you ain't got no whores down on the track, how in the hell are you goin' find out who's catchin' what and how?" Earl grinned at the other men, then added, "unless what you really mean is, let's ride down and see what them thoroughbred bitches I got are doing."

"Not really, Earl. You know you ain't the only person in this room who happens to have a soul sister working down on the track."

"Bravo, bravo!" Billy shouted, clapping loudly. Earl watched Billy with the attitude of a man well aware of the deceitful nature of the people he deals with.

Charles bent over and knocked the ashes off his joint. "Well, all the reefer is gone now, so let's do something."

"Here," Billy said, tossing a small package on the table. "Let's snort this little bit of poison up before we pull."

Earl stared at the package as though someone had tossed a snake on his table. "Well I'll be damned, Billy. You mean to tell me you've been carrying all that smack around in my car all day without me even knowing about it?"

"You didn't have nothing to worry about, Earl, and besides, it ain't nothing but a fifty-dollar bag," Billy answered.

Duke bent over the table and tore off a piece of

matchbox cover. He quickly creased the torn piece down the middle and stuck one end of the quill into the white powder. With an adept motion, he picked up some of the white powder with his quill and quickly stuck it into his nose. Snorting loudly, he looked around the small group. "What's the matter, baby," he said directly to Earl. "Is a little bit of money really making you get shitty?"

Earl spoke up sharply. "You can call it anything you want to, Duke, but I don't want you or Billy or any goddamn body in my house, car, or just in my company carrying no dope without me knowing about it!"

Charles tried to relieve the sting of Earl's words. "That's about the way Dicky-boy will feel about drugs by the time he gets out of prison," he said quietly.

His words put Billy on the defensive immediately. Everyone in the house knew just what he was saying. "What you're talking about ain't shit, Charles," Billy stated loudly. "That dope that was found in Dicky's car belonged to the white bitch, Pat. If he hadn't had the funky bitch sitting damn near in his lap, the dope wouldn't have been found at his feet."

There was a slight tightening of nerves, and the tension in the room could be felt. "Well, all of you were in the car together, my man," Earl said sharply, staring at Billy's flushed face. Before Billy could reply, Earl continued. "And I know for a fact that Dicky didn't fuck with no junk, so it sure didn't belong to him, and he's the one that got five years for it."

"That's bullshit and you know it!" Billy exploded. "They gave Dicky all that time because they knew he was driving a Cadillac that his white whores had bought for him. They been wantin' the man for years, and they got the chance and just socked it to him."

Earl stared around the room at the other men. He was young, strong, and full of confidence. "Well, that may be the case," he said, "but for the record, I want you to know that I don't want any drugs in my car unless you done pulled my coat to it."

"Aw, man, why you come up with that weak shit?" Billy asked, then added, "You act like I ain't got no Cadillac of my own, baby. I ain't just got to ride in yours."

"Well, you said it, Billy, I didn't. But since you stated it, I think that's the best thing I've heard. I know you ain't goin' do right, and every time you get in somebody's car, you're going to be carryin' some kind of drugs—for either you or your woman. So, you know, take your own weight."

"That's cool," Billy answered while in the process of snorting up some dope. "I guess you remember I left my car across town when I got in your car with you and Charles."

"You don't have to worry, Billy Banks," Earl replied. "I'm going to drop you and Duke back off at your car when we leave. I just want you to let me know when you get into my car if you're carrying dope on you. I like to be careful. I hate to have the police find a package of stuff on my floor when I don't really know how it got there."

The men stared at each other. Billy was far from being a fool, but he didn't really get angry over what Earl had said. If push came to shove, and he was in Earl's car and they got stopped, he knew in his heart that he'd stick the dope down in one of the cushions if he hadn't had the time to throw it out the window. Anything, just as long as he got rid of the dope so that the police couldn't take it out of his pocket. With the dope found in the car, he'd never have to worry about going to prison, not on a rap like that. Maybe Earl would end up losing his Cadillac, but that would be far better than getting a few years behind bars.

The phone rang, and since Charles was sitting right next to it, he got Earl's nod, then picked up the receiver.

"It's long distance, Earl," he said, holding the phone out as Earl reached for it.

"Hi, honey," Earl said, then hesitated and began to listen. He picked the phone up and started to walk away with it, but changed his mind. "What's the name of the doctor you're seeing?" he asked suddenly. He waited, then continued. "Well, if the doctor thinks you should go into the hospital, honey, then you do what he says. Female trouble can become a problem if you don't take care of it. How much money have you got? Four hundred.

Well, that should be enough. Get you a private room, and if the bill should run over that, let me know. But what you try and do is tell them you'll pay the rest, if it should turn out to be more than four hundred dollars. As soon as you get back to work, you should be able to take care of that yourself, Lill."

He nodded his head at something she said, then hung up. "The bitch done come down with female trouble," he said to no one in particular. Earl turned his back and walked over to the window and stared out. His mind was busy with how to handle the problem that had just come up. While his girl was in the hospital, he would miss the money that came regularly from the whorehouse in Pennsylvania, but the money wasn't his real problem. What he was pondering was whether or not he should send another girl up to fill the place of the one going to the hospital. If he did that, then when the one in the hospital got out, there would be confusion between the women. Lill was a good prostitute, but she couldn't get along with any of his other girls. That was one reason why he kept her working out of town. Whenever she came back to Detroit, she managed to always get into some kind of scrape with one of his other girls.

"Damn, baby," Duke said loudly. "You sure believe in blowing your money, don't you?"

Earl turned from the window and stared at him. "I don't know what you mean, man."

Duke smiled, revealing yellow spots on his teeth. "I mean by blowing all that money on a hospital bill. All you had to do was have her check in a general hospital somewhere, and when she got well, just leave. Ain't no way they can make a whore pay no bill." He grinned widely at his own cleverness. "Yeah, baby, if she was mine, I'd of had her mail that four hundred, maybe lettin' her keep fifty, or something like that. But she'd never have blown all that money for no doctor bill."

"Yeah, I see what you mean," Earl replied, then laughed harshly. "That's the difference in pimpin' and simpin', man. I let all my ladies go first class, all the time. That's why I got a stable of good young whores instead of some dopefiend bitches that shoot up all the profit."

"You can call it simpin' if you want to," Duke continued, determined to get his point across, "but I'd be four hundred bucks richer sometime today if I had been in your place."

"Fuck all that shit!" Billy said loudly, as he snorted up the rest of his dope. "I'd have asked you to take a blow, Charles, but I know you don't want your *big chief* Earl to know that you like a toot now and then." He glanced up at Earl, "Hey, man, how about running us back over on Johnny-R street so I can pick up my car?"

Earl picked up the vest that went with his mod walking suit. He walked into the bedroom to see if the brown silk outfit was fitting him properly.

When he came out, he was ready to go. The rest of the men got up and followed him to the door.

Billy laughed loudly as they walked out into the hallway. After closing the door and shaking it to make sure it was locked, Earl caught up with the group at the elevator. He spoke directly to Duke. "Everybody seems to have a lot of advice about how somebody else should treat their whores, but when it comes down to the real, all a nigger will find out is that all his so called friends have but one thought in mind, and that's how to steal one of them whores from his stiff ass if he lets his game get funny."

The elevator door opened in front of them. Earl stepped in before Duke could reply. There was an elderly, well-dressed couple already inside, so they discontinued the conversation.

2

AFTER DROPPING DUKE and Billy off, Earl, known in and out of all the craps-houses and after-hours joints in the city as "Earl the Black Pearl," decided to drive up on Twelfth and see what kind of action he could find on the corner so early in the evening. He didn't bother to ask the quiet man riding next to him if he wanted to go.

Slumped down in the front seat, Charles stared out of the wide Cadillac window. "You know what we should do for this coming holiday?" he asked suddenly, his voice a deep bass and seeming to rumble as he spoke.

"I don't know what we should do," Earl replied easily, "but I got a damn good idea of what I'm *going* to be doing." The news came on the radio, and Earl quickly switched on the tape recorder.

Charles stared at the slim, dark-skinned man

behind the steering wheel. Some black men seemed out of place behind· the wheel of the expensive automobiles they drove, wearing work clothes, factory outfits in a ten-thousand-dollar car, but Earl appeared as if the car had been made for him. The white on the white Cadillac fitted him to perfection. The diamonds that he wore glittered as his hand moved over and flicked the button to let down the electric window a crack. He lit up a stick of reefer. "That don't mean that I won't listen to a good idea for the coming holiday, though. Run it down, baby; I just might go for it."

"Naw, man, that's okay. It wouldn't have made no sense no way." Charles shrugged his shoulders and straightened up in the seat. "We just passed the Man coming out of that alley."

Earl nodded and continued to smoke the weed. Every now and then, he would check out the mirror. He started to speak, then caught himself. He didn't think he could get Charles to understand just what he meant, and he might just give the wrong impression. It was just that he got a nervous feeling whenever he passed policemen. It wasn't a fear; it was more like a danger signal. In them, he saw the constant threat to his way of life.

As he drove along, the neighborhood began its subtle change. He turned right on Twelfth, a one-way street, and pawnshops and nightclubs began to spring up on each side of the street. Farther on, one could see the devastation of the Sixties' burning and looting spree. It was everywhere. Here, a gutted building, next door, a large lot with the debris of past fires scattered over its barren surface.

They stopped for a red light, and the early evening breeze drifted lightly around the car. Everywhere they looked there were the clusters of people that the good weather brought out; they pushed against each other in the cluttered entrances of open doorways to apartment houses and poolrooms and shine parlors. Girls with shortened skirts stood in the darkened doorways, while their counterparts patrolled the sidewalks in revealing hotpants outfits.

Charles stared hungrily at one of the younger prostitutes.

"I'd bet money, Charles, that you'd turn a trick with that young girl if you wasn't 'shamed she'd come back up on the corner and tell it," Earl said, tossing back his head and laughing. It was a deep sound, one full of mirth, with the kind of heaviness coming through that aroused women. It was also a practiced laugh, one that could be turned on and off at will.

Charles joined in the laughter. He knew it was true. He'd never make a successful pimp of himself; he loved to groove too much. He fell in love with his woman's hips, and that love-joy was his downfall. Earl called it "having a tender dick."

"That's right, boy, you need to laugh," Earl said. "If there's any man who's guilty of following his dick, it's you. For a hard-on, Charles, you'll fuck around the drive five hundred goddamn miles, get there, get the cock, and never bother to ask about the trap money." He laughed again and stared at his husky partner. Charles was by nature a thug. He took his by wit or pistol. Ever since they were childhood friends, Charles was a strong-arm man. At that step in their development, Charles was the boy most of them looked up to. He was the fighter, going to the gym at night, taking up boxing.

How the worm turns, Earl thought coldly. He had been one of the cool ones during this period, always standing back against the wall, posing, and at all times as sharp as his wardrobe would allow him to be.

Another red light caught them. As they sat at the light, two brown-skinned girls crossed the street, flirting openly with the men in the Cadillac.

"Boy oh boy," Charles exclaimed. "You sure get a lot of action when you ride in a hog!"

Earl's laughter rang out sharp and clear. "It don't have to be the Caddie, baby; it just might have been me they were giving that action to, man."

"Shit!" Charles said loudly. "It was the Caddie, baby, that's what it was. Them bitches was lookin' at the ride. It wouldn't have made any difference if two apes was sitting in here!"

"Okay, baby," Earl replied easily. "I ain't about to start arguing over it with you, but one day you'll find out. It ain't always the car, but sometimes it helps out." He laughed again, this time softer.

16

Another red light caught them. As they sat waiting for it to change, a long, gold Eldorado turned the corner. The driver recognized Earl and blew the Eldorado's deep horn.

Earl waved at the driver. "Old Bobby Spencer," he said, speaking more to himself than to Charles. "That old man has handled more money than any four niggers in this city," he stated.

"I guess so," Charles answered. "If I had the good coke connect that he's got, I'd handle the same kind of money myself."

"Maybe. That man has been selling cocaine for over twenty years now, Charles, and he ain't got busted yet. Now that's what I call a smart street nigger."

"It ain't that he's all that smart, Earl, or that he can't get busted. He's just been lucky that them bitches that he's got dealing for him ain't never switched around on him and cracked him downtown. Shit, every time one of his broads gets busted, they take the weight themselves. Ain't none of them ever gave him no trouble." Charles fell silent, waiting for Earl to agree with him.

"That ain't luck, Charles, that's business. It shows the man knows what's happening. He must tell his women just how to handle it, 'cause if you don't explain it to a bitch and leave it to her to handle, she'll fuck it up every time."

Donald Goines

"I don't know," Charles mumbled. "It seems like luck to me. If it was me, the bitch would get downtown and tell it all."

"I'll agree with that," Earl said. "More than likely, you'd have left it up to the woman to handle it, never taking the time to sit her down and explain just what to tell them white folks downtown whenever the bust came. So when the bitch got busted, she'd be feeling on her own, and she'd try shifting the weight. It's all in being a top-notch player or just another mediocre-ass nigger out here in the streets."

After the exchange, they rode on in silence, neither man bothering to break the stillness. Each man sank down in his own thoughts, Charles thinking that he was right, that it was just a matter of luck, and Earl knowing that he was right, that it was just a matter of taking care of business. He saw a parking spot in front of a small barbecue restaurant, pulled over and let his white convertible-top down.

As the top went back slowly, four young girls standing in the front of the greasy spoon restaurant stared at the occupants of the car brazenly. In their glance, there was an invitation that needed no words to explain. The weather was warm, the evening was young, and a ride in a convertible would beat the hell out of standing in front of a dirty restaurant. The girls were more than eager. They were ready.

Without seeming to, Earl steadily examined the

women. Suddenly, there was a quick movement to his eyes as they focused on one of the girls in particular. "Hummmmmm," he murmured. "What a lovely creature that is."

Before he had time to make a move of his own, Charles took the play out of his hands. "Come here, baby," he yelled, not picking out any particular girl.

Two of the young girls moved away from the window and walked over to the car. The beauty that Earl had noticed was one of them. When the girls reached the car, Charles began to fidget. Now that the action was right in front of him, he was at a loss for words. Earl watched his friend, amused, and his lips turned down in a cold sneer that he was unconscious of.

The girls were amused by Charles' seeming inability to follow up on his bold approach. "Uh," he began, "uh, ain't you got a sister, girl, that works out of the honey-bunch bar?" he asked, trying the break the cold silence.

The tall brown-skinned girl, whom he had addressed the question to, put her hand on her hip. "No, baby, I'm afraid you've got me mixed up with somebody else." She answered frankly, her eyes shifting over to Earl. It was obvious that she wasn't interested in Charles.

The slight rejection stung Charles, and he became nasty. "Bitch, I ain't got you mixed up with nobody. Your sister is whoring out of the motherfuckin' bar, so you ain't got to lie about it!"

Now she gave Charles her full attention. She stared straight into his eyes and answered. "If I do have a sister working out of there at night, I don't see why you should be concerned with it, 'cause she sure ain't got no stiff-ass nigger like you for her man." She rocked back on her heels, spreading her legs so that the tight, tiny skirt seemed about to burst.

Earl caught his breath. My god, he thought and shook his head, she's lovely. With the sun shining down on her, she seemed to be a dark bronze, a golden rust color. Her skin had the same deep color of a shiny penny, deep with a darkish tan. He stared at her face. Her eyes, a midnight black, were flashing now that she was angry. Her small, well-developed nose seemed to swell as small beads of perspiration rolled from her brow. If there was any defect in her beauty, it was the small gap between her front teeth.

Deciding to break it up before it got out of hand, Earl laughed softly. "That's what you get for yelling at young girls, Charles; they haven't had a man sit them down and teach them how to really respect a man. So they might say anything." Earl's main concern had been to pacify Charles because he knew the large man had an uncontrollable temper at times, which could be very dangerous for anyone who opposed him—male or female.

His words aroused the girl's anger. She leaned over and pointed her finger at Earl. "Ain't that about a *bitch*!" she snarled. "I'm supposed to have been disrespectful." She laughed harshly. "Ain't that about a pound of pure shit! Here your friend calls me a bitch from out of a clear blue sky, and *I'm* disrespectful." She dragged the words out, still pointing her finger. "When he called me over to the car, I thought I was being called over to the car by a couple of players, but I see now what's happening. It's just like they say, you can take a nigger out of the country, but you can't get the country out of a nigger."

Her girlfriend nudged her, then tried to take her arm and pull her away. She shook the girl's arm off. "These niggers screamed on me first, honey; I didn't say nothing to them." She tossed her head angrily, making the natural long black hair whip about her shoulders.

Charles shook his head stupidly. The directness of the girl's attack left him completely dumbfounded. To make up for his first error, he now blundered straight ahead without thinking. "Bitch, if you don't know how to respect a man yet, a couple of well-placed punches upside your head will make you tighten your game so that you'll respect one in the future!"

The young girl stared at Charles as if he had lost his mind. Her girlfriend gave her arm one more pull, then split back to the safety of her other girlfriends. The sharp, unwavering stare made Charles more angry than he had been. He fumbled to open the car door. Earl was caught completely off guard by the quick turn of events.

Before Charles was out of the car, the girl had read his intentions. She ran around the car as Charles jumped from the front seat, and she stopped beside Earl's open window. "Listen, mister, my name is Vickie, and I didn't walk up to your car to get jumped on. Can't you do something with this crazy friend of yours?"

Before Earl could answer, Charles ran up and caught the girl by both arms. He shook her so violently her head jerked dangerously on her shoulders. Earl moved swiftly. The girl was in real danger, and he knew from experience that Charles was very unpredictable.

Pushing the steering wheel up and out of the way, he slid out of the car. He caught Charles' furious stare. He nodded towards the car seat. "I got just what she needs, baby boy."

His words seemed to take effect on the large man. "What you need is a man, bitch." Charles snarled, then pushed her into the open car.

As she tried to catch her balance, Charles slapped her viciously across the mouth. "Maybe Earl will take the time and teach you how to respect a man," he said as she sprawled out on the front seat.

Earl slid smoothly between the fighting couple, pushing the girl's legs out of the way as he got under the steering wheel. He grinned up at Charles. "Thanks, baby boy. You never really know about these things, but ain't no sense us going to jail tonight, is there, man?"

Before Charles could mutter a reply, the large motor in the car came alive. It roared deeply, sounding powerful. "You know, you can get busted jumping on young girls," Earl said. His loud laughter rang out, and he pulled away from the curb, leaving Charles standing in the middle of the street staring around stupidly.

It had been crude, he thought coldly to himself as he stared into his rearview mirror at Charles. Charles was a pain in the ass, Earl reflected for the thousandth time. Without glancing in the girl's direction, Earl leaned over and punched the tape recorder. In moments, the interior of the car was flooded with music.

"My name is Vickie." The short statement didn't seem to carry any hostility. Rather, the voice seemed more like a caress: intimate, deeply private.

This time Earl did glance around. He stared at her openly and was shaken. For the first time in his pimping life, a woman with nothing but her voice and appearance had made a strong impression on him.

After taking a sharp curve, Earl reached over and removed a box of tissue from his glove compartment. "Here, honey, your eyes got kind of wet back there. Maybe you can use some of these."

She removed a few from the box, then pulled the sun visor down and began repairing her makeup. "Your friend must be some kind of nut. Does he get his kicks from beatin' up people?"

"He did seem to get upset back there over

nothing, honey, but what he told you was true. You brought most of that down on yourself by your flip answers." Earl hesitated slightly, then continued. "I've known Charles for quite a while, and you can take my word for it, he ain't freakish to beatin' up folks, even though he does a damn good job of it if he ever gets started."

With a sudden toss of her head, Vickie laughed. "Well, I can chalk it up as a cheap lesson, plus, from now on—whenever, wherever, or however I come in near contact with your friend—I'll personally give him as much room as I would any dangerous animal I'd happen upon if I lived in a jungle."

She removed her eyebrow pencil and redid her shaved eyebrows. From what Earl had noticed, she was tall and well shaped for her age. She had the exceptional body of a young girl who hadn't had any babies yet, while her complexion had a golden hue about it—a compelling light brown, not as light as the average Spanish person, yet not as dark as many Latin people.

As she crossed her long, beautiful legs, Earl followed the motion with his eyes. "I'd like to ask you a few very personal questions, Vickie, but from the bell, I want you to know that I don't want any lies. Rather, if you will, try and explain whatever it is to me and the reason why you'd have lied to me about it, you understand?"

Slightly angered, she twisted in the seat, causing the tight black skirt she wore to rise up on her lovely thighs. "Well, I didn't know accepting a lift from you would cause me to have to submit a resume to you that I don't think is any of your business."

"Damnit," he cursed softly as a red light caught him in the middle of the street. He pushed the gas pedal down and ran the light. Both of them glanced back, looking for the ever-present police car at times like that.

"I'm sorry, Vickie, I really haven't explained myself to you, so I can understand your misunderstanding my approach." Before she could say anything, he continued. "I really don't want to know a hell of a lot about you, but there is one thing I want to know, and I want the truth. How old are you?"

Now it was her turn to hesitate. "I'm not ashamed because I'm young, nor do I have any reason to lie about it." Vickie turned and stared up at him, and the lie that she was about to state died on the tip of her tongue. "I'm only seventeen. My next birthday is next year, too." Now why in the hell did I go and do that, she scolded herself harshly. I could have told him eighteen and he'd never have known the difference.

"I had put you on being seventeen, girl. Is there somewhere I can drop you off?"

Vickie was startled. "If you thought I was seventeen, Earl, and that's too young, why did you go through the bother of pulling away from the curb with such a baby in your car?" She stared at him with all the brashness of youth.

Earl returned her stare. She was pretty, all right, but she represented a problem. The way he lived demanded that the woman pay her own way. He couldn't afford to support her. "I'll be honest with you, girl, I was hopin' that you was eighteen or would be turning that age soon."

Without anger, she began to speak, her voice was low and husky. "I don't go to school, Earl. I quit when I was sixteen and started working downtown in a restaurant with my mother."

She had his attention now. Mainly because she seemed sincere. She seemed to be much more mature than her age warranted. He thought about her until she broke the silence.

"I moved away from home last week when my mother brought my new stepfather home. He can't keep his hands off me."

He studied her closely, wondering how much of this he could really believe. He knew from experience that a young girl might tell him anything. "Where are you staying at now?" he asked, still not committing himself.

"I've been staying with different girlfriends every night. I checked my bags down at the Greyhound bus station. That way I don't have no problem whenever I want to change clothes. The locker don't cost but a dime a day."

"Talkin' about a temporary arrangement, you

really got one, Vickie," he said quietly. It was already in the back of his mind to do whatever he could to add this young devil to his stable. "It's no doubt about it, baby, you do need help, but the problem is really whether or not you will accept it."

She knew just what he meant. She was far from being a naive young girl. Vickie was well aware of what pimps did for a living. She rode on in silence, watching the landscape as he sped through the city streets.

Earl parked in front of his apartment building, and Vickie followed along silently as he got out and led the way through the lobby and into the elevator. It was a smooth, quick ride to the upper penthouse floor. The elevator deposited them in the hallway, and while Earl searched for his key, Vickie stared around in astonishment at the elegance. He opened the door and stepped back, allowing her to enter the suite before him. She stopped and stared around dumbfounded.

It was the first time in her life she had ever seen anything like his penthouse apartment outside of a movie. The extra-thick, dark red wall-to-wall carpet gave her the sensation of sinking every time she took a step. The furnishings were French provincial, rich, ornate, and colorful. The bedroom doors were modern French doors, with two adjoining doors hinged at the sides to open in the middle and long glass sidepanes that were stained so that they matched the rest of the expensive decor.

"Damn, baby," he said lightly. "Every time I bring a black girl up here she acts like she has stepped into another world." He grinned as she drew herself up.

His remark irritated her and she replied acidly, "Oh? If that's the case, then I'd take it for granted that all of your girls must be lily white—or real damn light."

Earl smiled, "Pull your horns in, baby. To be honest, I don't have any white girls, not at the present anyway. All of my ladies are soul sisters, Vickie."

The tension that had begun to build between them disappeared, and Vickie relaxed once again. "I'm glad to hear that," she said. "I'd rather have a dozen wife-in-laws, if they're black, than one ofay."

Earl studied her closely before replying. He had just about chosen her, but he wanted to be sure. "Being a whore, Vickie, is more than just a notion. It's not like what you see in the movies, where a girl spends all day and half the night with a john, and then puts on airs about receiving the cash. Out there in the streets, you get your money quick, real quick, girl." He snapped his fingers to illustrate.

Vickie laughed, a deep, husky sound. It was full of life and joy. "You jump to conclusions fast, don't you, Earl? I haven't even said anything about wanting to be a whore, but yet you've taken it for granted." The sound of her laughter was rich and carried a note of excitement in it.

Earl walked over to the bar and mixed himself a drink. He stared at her for a long time before answering. "It's possible I could have made a mistake, Vickie, but I doubt it. I don't think you have been wasting my time, or yours either." He smiled slightly. "Now, if you want to play coy or something like that. . . ." He shrugged his well-shaped shoulders, and the muscles rippled under his silk shirt. "Don't tell me I've really wasted my time bringing you up here," he said, half amused. The lights flickered on her raven black hair, and he idly wondered how she would look in a loud, blonde wig. She really didn't need one, he reflected, answering his own question.

Vickie reached across the bar and laid her hand on top of his. She stared into his deep black eyes. "Damn, baby," she said softly. "You don't believe in giving a woman very much time to make up her mind, do you?"

His laughter rang out loudly. He waved his hand around, indicating their surroundings. "You have to work your way up to something like this, Vickie. A girl in a fifty-dollar-a-week job couldn't begin to expect to live in such a place."

"If other women can afford to live in such a place," Vickie replied, putting her hands on her hips, "I don't see why I can't make the grade."

"It's possible," he answered. "But every bitch don't live in no penthouse just because she sells a little ass. Only the very best whores are qualified to live in this kind of joint. Some whores catchin' all their lives and still can't get out of a cold-water flat." He waited, watching her reaction before adding, "It's not just the looks that count, honey. A girl can be beautiful, just like you are, and built up like the famous brick shit house, but if she happens to be lazy or really scared, she won't ever make any money that will amount to anything."

Vickie lit a cigarette, slowly inhaled, then blew the smoke out over her head. "How can you tell a good girl? I mean, how can you tell a real good hustler from one that's just fair?"

"That ain't no problem. A thoroughbred always stands out, honey. The would-be thoroughbred will fade in the stretch, but the pedigreed mud-kicker, she'll come up catchin' them *big* every time."

"In other words, Earl, you can just about look at a woman and you can tell if she's going to be a winner or not?"

"No, baby, I didn't say that. I don't know how I gave you that impression. When it comes to a good thoroughbred whore, the only way you judge is by the money. An average bitch will go out in the streets and work hard as hell 'til she gets fifty dollars, then she'll end up bullshitting the rest of the night because she'll think she done made enough for her night's trap."

"You ain't bullshittin' me, are you, Earl?" Vickie asked, surprised. "Fifty or sixty dollars sounds like a lot of money to me—for just one night's work. Especially if you make that much every night." She stared at him curiously, wondering if he was just playing the big shot with her. She knew she was young, and there were a lot of things she didn't know, but fifty dollars added up to quite a bit of money in the run of a week if you made that much every night. Shit, she thought, in the run of a week, you'd have made close to five hundred dollars. And to her way of thinking, five hundred dollars was a whole lot of cash.

Without any form of humor, Earl stated dryly, "It ain't shit, woman! That's why I say only the very best of hustling girls get a chance to live like this." Again he waved his hand around, taking in the apartment. "Fifty dollars a day wouldn't even pay the rent on this place, Vickie. You have to think *big,* honey, if you want to do big things."

Vickie sat down on a bar stool and stared at Earl coldly. "I don't care what it takes, daddy, but if another black bitch can do it, I'm ready and willing to start learning. And," she added, "I mean to be one of the very best."

"Good," Earl said. He walked from behind the bar and opened the bedroom door. "Since you feel like that, you might as well start learning now."

Her eyes followed him as he entered the bedroom. I knew it, she told herself silently as she got up and followed him into the bedroom. I thought pimps were different, she thought coldly, but when it comes down to the nitty-gritty, they have the same thing on their fuckin' minds as the rest of the men. That's all any of them really have on their minds, just what does it take to get this bitch in bed. Well, I've made my choice, so I guess I'll have to follow it to the end, she reasoned, closing the bedroom door behind her. She removed her sweater and slowly undid the buttons on her blouse. She removed the garment and laid it neatly on a chair. With a swift motion, she raised her skirt and removed her garter belt. In a moment, she was completely nude, revealing all of her natural beauty.

Earl stared at her coldly. She was a very attractive girl, and he knew that her youth would be an asset on the open market. He turned his back on her and removed a towel from the large mahogany dresser that covered most of the north wall. "Here," he said, tossing the towel to her. "Take a bath. It might cool you off." He smiled. "You'll find all the bath oils and whatever else you might need in the medicine cabinet."

Vickie caught the towel and glared angrily. "I may have been poor, but I was able to take a bath every day, so I don't think I'm carrying any kind of odor."

"I don't doubt that at all, Vickie. In fact, I wasn't thinking about you smelling or anything like that when I made the suggestion. I just happen to have some outfits I want you to try on, and I'm so used to taking a shower before I put on anything new, I thought that you probably had the same habit when it came to new clothes."

"You're right about that," she answered, breaking into a quick smile. "I'm sorry if I sounded a little peeved. A bath would make me feel a hundred percent better, too." She quickly wrapped the towel around her and started towards the bath.

Earl caught up with her at the door. He caressed one of her lovely golden brown breasts. "Your tit is as hard as a rock. It won't take a trick long to figure out that he's getting something young and tender," Earl said, leaning down and running his tongue gently over one of her nipples until it became rigid.

She tossed her head back as a smothering light came into her eyes, and her breathing became harsh as he kissed her in the deep curve of her neck.

Earl pushed her back and held her at arm's length. "Damn!" he exclaimed. "I'd better let you go on and take care of your business, or won't nothing get done." He twisted her around and spanked her on the ass playfully as he shoved her towards the bath. "Oh, by the way, baby," he said, "what size dress do you wear?"

3

EARL SAT BACK ON THE BED and listened to the water run in the shower. Suddenly a voice came over the telephone he held in his hand. "Is that you, Connie?" he asked as he made himself comfortable.

"Yes, daddy, it's me. I've been sitting here trying to reach you all day on the phone, honey. I'd just about given up on catchin' up with you today, daddy."

Earl smiled to himself. "That just goes to show you, Connie, that all good things come to those who wait."

Connie giggled happily over the phone. "Earl, when am I going to see you, baby? You ain't even bothered to pick up your money from me in the last four days." She tried to sound offended.

There was a small distraction as Vickie came

out of the bathroom. Earl watched her as she emerged, wearing a transparent shortie gown. He removed the receiver from his ear and pointed towards the dresser. "Try a dab of that After Five, Vickie, and let me know how you like it," he ordered before resuming his phone conversation.

"Listen, Connie, I want you to have your maid transfer all your dates that call tonight over to Fay's." He had to interrupt Connie before she could complain. "Just listen, woman, until I get through talking! You might learn something if you shut your goddamn mouth long enough to hear."

"Okay, daddy," she replied meekly. His voice drowned out the rest of her words.

"After I hang up, Connie, you call Fay and tell her I said to handle your tricks for the next day or two. After you do that, I want you to bring me a couple of your After-Five dresses over here, with a pair of matching heels. You do wear a size seven, don't you?"

"What, size seven shoes or dress, daddy?" She asked facetiously. She smiled as she visualized Earl frowning angrily.

Earl sat up on the bed. "Bitch! What the fuck's wrong with you? You know damn well you can't get your wide black ass in no size seven dress, so stop playing games with me!"

"Well, I just asked," she muttered. "You don't have to get upset about it, do you?"

He cooled down slightly. "Well, don't be asking me nothing silly. Now, you get on the case and take care of my business, and get that shit on over here as soon as possible. Oh yeah," he added after a slight hesitation, "you might as well bring me that bread since you're coming. And also, Connie, be sure to dress so that you'll be ready to go to work tonight."

"Yes, daddy," she mumbled as the phone went dead in her ear. She stared at the wall silently for a minute. then jumped up and started getting ready.

Vickie lay down on the bed beside Earl and rubbed up against him. Earl slid off the other side of the bed and began to remove his shirt. Vickie stared at him quietly. She noticed that his chest was completely bare of hair. He placed his shirt on a hanger and hung it on a small rack. After that, he removed a large roll of money from his pants pocket and placed some bills in his wallet. The rest of the money he left lying on the dresser.

"Vickie, I'm going to try and teach you how to peel," Earl stated as he tossed the wallet onto her lap.

She picked up the wallet and started to examine it. Earl leaned down and, using only his little finger and thumb, reached into the wallet and removed two twenty dollar bills.

"Did you see how I did that?" he asked her quietly as he stared down into her dark eyes. Vickie nodded and tried to duplicate the act. Four or five large bills fell out on the bed as the wallet slipped from her grasp.

"Keep trying," Earl said lightly as he watched her closely. He watched her with keen interest for about fifteen minutes before he reached over and removed the wallet from her hands. For another five minutes, he demonstrated, showing her where she was using too many fingers and how to overcome this slight error. With the utmost patience, Earl placed the wallet back into her hands and watched her every move. Again he removed the wallet from her and stood up, but this time he placed the wallet in his back pocket. He undid the zipper of his pants.

Vickie watched him out of half-closed eyes. She was tired of the practice and unconsciously she spread her legs wider as she stretched her arms out over her head and lay out on the bed. She began to feel relief as she imagined the practice was over.

Earl pushed his pants down around his hips and climbed into the bed. Quickly he knelt between Vickie's outspread legs, then braced himself with his elbows, his hands on her breasts.

Vickie moaned lightly and placed her hands on his naked chest.

"Not up there, fool!" he snapped impatiently before he could catch himself. "Try getting the damn wallet without me feeling it."

"Oh," she moaned surprised, then blushed from head to toe, as she glanced up into his eyes. She couldn't see anything but cold, chilling icicles in the look he gave her, and she turned her head away.

Earl worked and worked with her in this posi- tion until sweat dripped from his body. The doorbell began to chime, breaking the boredom of the steady work. Earl slid off the bed gracefully. He gave her a friendly slap on the rear before walking out of the room to answer the door.

She stared after him in amazement. Never before in her short life span had she encountered a man like him. Never had a man treated her with so much indifference. When she had made up her mind to choose Earl, she had taken for granted the fact that they would end up in the bed that evening. Now, after being in bed with him for over an hour, he still hadn't taken advantage of what she had been offering. It was confusing, but in a way it was too good to be true. Here was a man who really had more on his mind than just how to get her in the bed. It was a beautiful change for once, she reasoned. She wondered briefly if he might be queer and didn't really have a need for a woman. Just as quickly, she discarded the notion as she remembered that he was supposed to have a stable full of women.

Earl entered the room, followed closely by a tall black woman.

"This is Connie," he said, pointing back over his shoulder. "And that's Vickie," he said, nodding towards the bed.

Connie stared down at the girl sprawled out on the bed. She had noticed Vickie's nakedness, and anger rose up in her quickly. "Some bitches have all the luck," she said angrily, her eyes flashing at Earl.

"Here," she said, handing a roll of money to him. She watched him anxiously as he counted the money out slowly. "I had over three hundred for you, daddy, but I had to pay the maid this morning," she said defensively.

Earl nodded silently as he finished counting the money. He tossed the money on the dresser beside his other bankroll.

"You ain't mad about the size of my trap, are you, baby?" she asked nervously.

He turned around and put his full stare on her. "For a four-day trap, Connie, I've seen a hell of a lot better ones than this. And from you, Connie." He continued to stare at her until she dropped her eyes. "You know yourself, Connie, that this ain't up to standard, even after I count what you paid the maid."

Connie had a habit of speaking fast when excited, and now words poured out. "Wait a minute, daddy, you're forgetting you told me to pay the rent out of the money the first part of this week. And don't forget the phone bill, too, daddy. I paid that, too." She smiled now.

He smiled with her. "Oh yeah, I had forgot all about them things, baby, so that takes care of the gap. I knew something was wrong, honey, 'cause your money ain't never been *that* short."

Vickie sat up on the edge of the bed. "Well, I'm glad she arrived. If she hadn't, my hands would be numb by now," she said, rubbing her hands together.

Not understanding, Connie stared at her as if she were losing her mind. Earl laughed. "I've been trying to teach her how to dip, Connie," he said by way of explanation.

"Oh yeah," Connie answered, beginning to understand. "It does take a lot of practice to really get it right."

"You might as well finish where I left off, Connie," Earl ordered, as he bent down and picked up a cigarette.

"That's okay with me," Connie said as she handed a bag to Vickie. "Here, honey, after you put some of these clothes on, I'll take you out on the streets and let you get some on-the job training."

Earl removed his bathrobe from the closet. "I should run into you ladies sometime this morning before you're through work, but in case I don't, Connie, I want you to take Vickie on home with you. I'll get in touch with both of you, so don't try and reach me unless it's very urgent. You understand?" He walked over to the door leading to the bath, then stopped. "Oh yeah, Connie, you better get her some fake identification. Make sure it makes her over twenty-one. We don't want any

trouble out of them policewomen downtown if
she gets busted."

"Don't worry about it, daddy," Connie replied
quickly. "If this bitch has any sense at all, by the
time I get through running it down to her, the police won't have no game at all to run down to this
fast sister."

Vickie quietly listened to them discuss her as
she slowly removed the clothes from the bag Connie had brought. With the indulgence of a woman
who has seen everything, Connie openly watched
Vickie dress. Her eyes never left the young woman's
body. "You and I might have to play house one of
these days, Vickie," she said in a husky voice.

Her words caused Vickie to twist around and
stare up at the woman who had been talking to
her. Vickie was tall, but next to Connie she was at
a disadvantage. The tall black woman towered
over her by inches. Connie was tall and muscu-
larly built. With her hands on her hips, she looked
like the black queen of the Amazons. "Why?"
Vickie asked sharply as she stood up to her full
height. "Is that supposed to go along with the
program, too?" Her eyes seemed to glitter as
anger flashed in them.

"No, it's an added attraction, honey, just a little
something that you might enjoy. You can call it a
way to kill too much energy."

Vickie laughed deeply as she ran her hands
down her voluptuous body straightening out the
short skirt she had put on. Her anger disappeared

quickly as she replied, "You know what they say. Women will be women, won't they?" The open invitation was there, and both women knew it. The sound of both of the women's merry laughter rang out and mingled as they left the room arm in arm.

Earl watched them depart, pleased with his brand new cop. It wouldn't take long at all, he reasoned, for her to catch on. Not long at all.

4

AFTER TAKING A HOT SHOWER and then shaving, Earl began to feel refreshed. He had worked up a sweat teaching Vickie how to dip. He took his time selecting a suit from the dozens that hung in his well stocked closet. After a long hesitation, he selected a dark blue silk suit and laid it across the bed. He walked back to the closet and removed a pair of midnight-blue suede shoes from his shoe rack. He then stopped at the dresser and removed a light blue silk shirt and matching tie. He took just as much trouble dressing as a woman would, slow and meticulous. He applied his cologne with an excessive amount of care. Silk shorts followed with a silk undershirt. After finally dressing, he examined his handiwork in the full length mirror. He straightened his diamond stick-pin twice before being satisfied, then went on to his hat rack. It took him fifteen minutes to become satisfied with the way the Dobbs Fifty fit his head. He tilted the short-brimmed hat slightly towards his forehead. The clock began to chime, and he counted the sounds as he went out. It was midnight on the nose as he stepped through the door on his way into the streets for the night.

It was a beautiful night. The stars were bright overhead and he was tempted to let the top down on his drop-top. Earl parked his car in front of the Top Hat nightclub and got out. The place was semi-crowded as he entered. He weaved his way through the tables, waving at different acquaintances sitting around the room.

Sister, a heavyset, brown-skinned woman, was behind the bar serving drinks. She spotted Earl coming between the tables and yelled to him good naturedly. "All these would-be pimps in here had better hide their tender young whores they claim, 'cause a real pimp done eased up on the set," she said, beaming at Earl.

Earl grinned at her and pointed up and down the bar. "I'm making everybody's counterfeit, Sister, from now on. When I tell you to bring me my tab, then they can go back to spending their own."

Sister laughed as she poured drinks for everybody at the bar. "I wish I had the money you pimps come in here and blow," she stated while wrapping a towel around a champagne bottle. With the expert motion of a pro bartender, she popped the cork without shooting it from the bottle. Then she shook ice cubes around in two glasses before setting one down in front of Earl.

Down the bar, a short, middle-aged man banged loudly with an empty beer bottle. "What the goddamn hell's the matter around here," he yelled loudly, "can't a man get some service in this fuckin' place?"

Sister turned around and glared at him coldly. "If you don't watch that language, you won't get nothing else in this place!"

"Well, hurry up, then. It don't take all night, do it?" he replied, some of the heat going out of his voice. He removed a dollar bill from his pocket and waved it in Sister's direction. "Give this cute little girl what she wants to drink," he said, pointing to a young prostitute sitting next to him.

The young woman looked at the dollar and wrinkled her nose. "Don't worry about me, Sister, I wouldn't know what to order with all that bread he's spending," she said.

With a smooth motion, Sister picked up the dollar and put it in her bra. "Don't worry about it, Doris, Earl's buying the drinks for the next few rounds, anyway."

As the night wore on, couples began to drift into the club. Most were mixed, as prostitutes began to arrive with two, and sometimes three or more white men.

Billy entered the bar, followed closely by Duke. He waved at Earl but continued on towards the end of the bar where two prostitutes sat drinking alone. Pat, a frail blonde with red freckles on her nose, moved over to make room. Billy slid in between the two women.

"I guess you and Preaches already know each other, don't you, Billy?" she asked, nodding towards the girl named Preaches. Her voice was shrill.

"No, Pat, baby, I don't think me and Preaches really know each other," he stated and stared boldly at the tiny white girl sitting beside him. She squirmed under his cold stare. Preaches blushed as he continued to stare. She tossed her head back, shaking the long red hair out of her face.

"We have never really met," Preaches managed to say, "but we seem to always run into each other at the after-hours places, or at one of the bars."

Billy grinned at the cute little redhead. "You've been noticing the Hammer, ain't you, baby? All you broads be peepin' at the Hammer whenever he shows up, don't you?" His voice was loud as he referred to himself. He pinched her arm lightly. "You know heavy game when you see it, don't you, girl?"

"That's right, baby," she said quickly. "The real will come out."

Duke spoke up from the other side of the table. "Where's that little skinny boy you mess with, Red? Don't tell me he's scared to come out where the big fellers are at, is he?"

Preaches glanced at Duke. "Maybe that's the reason I'll never choose another small man again,

STREET PLAYERS

and I'm not talking about size, either," she stated harshly.

Billy raised his eyebrows. "You're talking like a big girl now, baby. You know when a man handles big money, if he has anything on the ball, he can pick and choose his ladies."

Pat turned around on her chair. "If a bitch is qualified to get big money, I don't care if a nigger has got two big dope bags, he'll accept good whore money," she said.

There were sarcastic overtones in Billy's voice as he laughed. "Bitch," he said, "what the hell are you talking about? You make good money, but after you make a hundred dollars, by the time you get out of the dopehouse, you ain't got ten dollars left."

Sister came down the bar and opened a bottle of champagne for Billy. As she stood there. Pat answered him. "I'm not one of those funky-ass black bitches out in the streets trying to steal twenty dollars," she stated maliciously. "I can go into any hotel in the city—not the city, nigger, but the *world*—and work. So I don't have to worry about what I shoot up."

"Well, this ain't no hotel, Pat," Sister informed her angrily. She placed her hands on her hips and continued. "And furthermore, while you're in this bar, try watching your dirty mouth or take your goddamn business elsewhere!"

Before Pat could answer, Billy spoke up. "All

right, Sis, we just got a little carried away, so don't give us no sermon, please."

"Humph!" Sister snorted, then stomped back down the bar, muttering to herself. She stopped in front of Earl and said loudly, "You know, niggers ain't shit!"

Earl stopped whispering to the young girl, Doris, who was sitting on the bar stool next to him. He glanced up at Sister in surprise. "I don't know what makes you say that, Sis. You're stepping on my toes with a blanket indictment like that."

"All you pimps are the same, Earl. Put you niggers around some tramp-ass white bitch, and all of you will sit there and let them use nigger this and nigger that." She raised her hands in a hopeless gesture, then continued. "I've got my first time to see one of you check one of them white whores, but on the other hand, let one of these white men sitting in here use the word nigger, and we'd have to call out the riot squad to keep ya'll from killin' him."

Before Earl could reply, Sister walked back up the bar, shaking her large hips. Earl glanced down the bar at Billy. Billy tossed up both hands in the sign of surrender.

"You know how evil some of these soul sisters can get," he yelled down the bar at Earl. "Maybe her old man ain't givin' her enough beef at night."

Earl grinned and picked up the empty champagne bottle in front of him. Sister came back down the bar and stopped. She banged his bar bill down in front of him loudly. He glanced quickly at the ninety-four dollar bar tab, took his roll out and pulled off a hundred dollar bill and a crisp twenty, and tossed both bills on the bar. "Pop me another one of those champagnes, baby, then you take that bullshit you got going down to the other end of the bar, 'cause me and Doris ain't said nothing to make you mad."

Sister turned and rang the money up. The fat, bald headed man that Doris had been sitting with earlier pushed his way drunkenly between them. His voice was harsh and his breath carried a strong odor as he said, "Now that I've done spent all my money buying you drinks, you goin' come down here and sit with this slick-ass nigger?" He stared at Earl belligerently.

Without replying, Earl grabbed his fresh bottle of champagne and glass and slid off the stool. "Maybe I should have stayed at home in bed, 'cause this sure don't seem like this is my night,' he said as he started to walk away, headed towards Billy.

"You better damn well bet this ain't your night," the drunk yelled stupidly as he climbed up on the vacated stool.

Big Joe, the bouncer, caught Earl's eye as he walked past. The bouncer nodded in the direction of the drunk. He knew the big spenders from the once-a-month bottle of beer customers that came to the bar, and Mike, the dago who owned the place, catered to the pimps and whores who came in regularly.

Earl shrugged his shoulders. "He's just drunk, Joe. If he don't bother me any more than that, I'll act like he never spoke to me."

It didn't sit that lightly with Doris. After getting away from the drunk once, she had no intention of being pawed over again. "Listen, mister," she said angrily, "you ain't spent a fuckin' thing on me tonight, and if you had, didn't nobody twist your arm and make you buy me any drinks."

The drunk muttered angrily and grabbed Doris by the arm. She tried to slide off the stool, but he twisted her wrist. Her eyes glittered dangerously as she removed a switchblade from her bra. The drunk, still unaware of his danger, attempted to pull the woman towards him.

There was a sudden silence as the people in the room could smell the danger that was about to be released. Doris's face was twisted in an involuntary contraction of pain. The muscles stood out in her high cheekbones, but she didn't cry out as the drunk attempted to twist her arm around and behind her back. She flowed with the motion. As the drunk pulled her towards him, she came up tight against him, and the knife flashed once. As fast as the bouncer had moved, he was still too late. The trick grunted in pain, then screamed at the top of his voice.

Joe reached the struggling couple first and

grabbed the trick back before she could stab him again. Earl grabbed Doris from behind. "Come on, baby, you done blowed this scene. We got to get the fuck out of here."

Her eyes still glittered dangerously, but she followed him quickly from the bar.

5

THE EVENING SEEMED to have flown past to Vickie as she paced up and down her selected working location. She felt in her bra to make sure the money was still in place. So far, it had been a good night. As she stood on the corner, a Caddie pulled up. The driver had a high natural. Vickie turned her back to him and walked away. Another car pulled up and stopped. She glanced over her shoulder as Connie called out to her from the open car window.

"Hey, Red! Come on and ride with me for a minute." She didn't wait for an answer; she just opened the car door. Vickie hopped in and glanced curiously at the white driver. His eyes lit up in obvious appreciation of the golden brown woman who had just got in.

"Well, sweetie, let's not just sit here while you

gape at my friend," Connie said. "Start up and make a right turn at the next corner." She gave him his directions and had him park in a dark alley. He twisted around in the seat, completely ignoring the woman whom he had picked up first. "How much would it cost for you and me to do a little business, Red?" he asked, using the same name he had heard Connie use.

"It won't cost you but twenty-five dollars, honey," she purred sweetly. He cursed. "I don't want to buy you," he said, "I just want to buy a piece of tail. You charge twice as much as your friend does."

Vickie shrugged her shoulders. "Sweetie, I didn't get in your car to argue with you, and besides, you happen to be my girlfriend's date, so I don't really want to do anything with you."

The trick grumbled. "Ass is ass to me." But his actions belied the very words he spoke. He couldn't take his eyes from Vickie. As she made a motion to get out of the backseat, the short skirt she wore slid up higher on her hips. He stared openly and, as the golden brown thighs flashed before him, his mouth began to water. Vickie watched the trick, amused. She had learned a lot in her short time on the street.

"Wait a minute! Just you hold your horses," the john managed to say as he fumbled with his wallet. He pulled his money out and climbed over the seat. Connie watched him stuff the wallet back in his pocket. She was hurt because Vickie got the trick who had been hers in the first place. Since the money was going the same place, it didn't make any difference who turned the john. The only thing it did was save her the trouble of having to put up with the goddamn trick, she thought. For that she was thankful.

The john was breathing heavily as he pushed the money into Vickie's hands. He ran his hands up and down her legs as she gave the money to Connie to hold. He glared at Connie as if he were seeing her for the first time. "What are you gonna do, girl, wait outside the car until we get through?" he said harshly.

"Hell no!" Connie said, turning her back on the couple and starting to fumble with the radio.

Without hesitating, the john ignored the woman in the front seat after that. He was too busy with Vickie. He pulled her roughly towards him. Vickie put her hands on his chest and pushed back. "Take it easy, honey, we're going to take care of business, but rushing ain't goin' help matters at all." She laughed, taking the sting out of her words, then asked, "How would you like it, sweetie, French style? It would blow your mind."

"Fuck that shit," the trick said. "I like it the old-fashioned way. Just give me a plain old lay."

Vickie was all business now. She quickly unbuttoned his pants and moved her fingers expertly until he was fully aroused. He attempted to push her hands away, but she continued. She made him pull his pants and shorts down around his hips, as she slid under him. Because of his large pot belly, he had a difficult time getting on top of her. She pulled her short skirt up around her stomach. Under the skirt she wore nothing. Panties only got in the way. She managed to help him insert the tiny penis. The trick grunted like a fat red pig as they began the act of copulation.

Now Vickie became very busy. Her fingers moved expertly as she removed his wallet. The practice really paid off. Connie reached down and got the wallet out of her hand. She moved fast, removing the money in one smooth motion. She could tell from the trick's grunts that he wouldn't last another second. With precise movements, she checked the wallet for hidden compartments before putting it back into Vickie's waiting hand. Vickie replaced the wallet with ease.

She twisted her mouth away as the john reached his climax and attempted to kiss her. "None of that shit," she said, slipping from under him. The trick looked surprised and hurt as her voice changed from that of a sweet-talking girl to that of a hard, harsh speaking whore.

"What's wrong, girlie?" he asked jokingly. "Didn't I make it good enough for you?" It was asked in a joking manner, but in his voice was the need to be told that he was good—at least as good as the rest of the men she did business with. He seemed to hold his breath as he waited for her reply.

Vickie didn't even bother to answer. Connie pushed some toilet paper into her hand as she climbed out of the car and attempted to clean herself up. The trick felt for his wallet as both the women left the car. Feeling it in place, he began to button up his clothes. Connie tossed him some toilet paper. "Use this, honey," she said, not unkindly. "You don't want your wife to find out how naughty you've been behaving, do you?" Before the john could reply, both girls had disappeared behind the car into the darkened alley. He squinted into the darkness, not quite believing that the women could have left that quickly. One minute they were there, and the next they were both gone.

Connie led the way across the alley between two darkened houses that appeared deserted. She moved fast, with Vickie trotting to keep up. After reaching a side street, she glanced up and down before attempting to cross it. They crossed and entered another alley, walked down it a short distance, then cut through another yard. Connie continued leading at a fast pace until they were a good four blocks away from where they had started.

"Damn, Connie," Vickie managed to whisper. "Can't we slow down some?" She clutched at her side, where a sharp pain had suddenly hit her.

"Not yet," Connie answered, then grabbed her by the arm and pulled her along. "When that trick misses his money, he's going to start riding this neighborhood until daybreak lookin' for nobody else but our little sweet asses. And you can bet money, baby, that he's going to cover more ground than us in that car."

Before she had finished speaking, a car slowed down beside them, giving both women a scare. They stared at the young white face peering out at them. Connie went to work immediately. "Wait a minute, honey," she yelled, bending down in the famous whore stance, hands on hips, legs spread invitingly. The car came to a stop in the middle of the street. With care, Connie approached the car, glancing up and down the side street to make sure no other car was coming. Assured, she walked around the car and stopped at the driver's window.

The young man inside the car rolled down the window halfway and asked in a southern drawl, "Well, where ya gals goin' this time of the mornin'?"

"How about giving us a lift to the west side, mister?" Connie asked flirtingly, rolling her tongue out provocatively. She watched the gleam come into the man's eyes, well aware of his intentions.

"By god, yes, gal. I was a goin' down thataway to see what I could find anyway," His voice died down to a whisper as Vickie ran out from the shadows where she had been hiding. At Connie's beckoning, she ran over and jumped in the car beside Connie, who had climbed in first and snuggled up close to the driver. She placed her hand intimately on the man's leg as he drove.

The hillbilly reached under the car seat and removed a fifth of whiskey. He took a large drink from the bottle, then pushed the bottle towards Connie. "Come on, hon, take a little swig, gal. I been ridin' and lookin' for me some dark meat all night," he said in his southern drawl.

His voice irked Vickie. She turned from the window and stared at the red-faced man. "How much money did you say you was willing to spend, honey?" she asked, and her voice was velvet smooth, not showing any of the hostility she felt.

He twisted around and stared drunkenly at her for a second. "I ain't got but seven dollars, gal," he said, then added harshly. "And that's five dollars too much."

Vickie's laughter was cold. "That's why your poor ass has been ridin' all fuckin' night!" Before she could add anything else, Connie hit her in the side with an elbow.

"Honey, I just know an old farm boy like you would, and could, spend ten dollars on some of this good black pussy, now couldn't you, big fellow?" Connie asked sweetly.

His next move took both women by surprise. The hillbilly slammed on the brakes and pulled to the curb. "By god!" he screamed at the top of his voice, "I said I ain't got but seven dollars! Now if you fuckin' whores don't want that, you can get your goddamn asses out."

Vickie started to open the car door, but Connie grabbed her arm. "I didn't say I wouldn't take seven dollars, honey," she purred, "just drive on.

The hotel's four blocks down that away." She
pointed to her left.

He pulled the car from the curb and slid his
hand down between her legs, grinning all the
while. "By god, I really likes you, gal, you know
that?"

Connie closed her legs tightly so that his hand
couldn't reach up too far under her skirt. "Turn
left at the next corner, sweetie," she directed the
driver. They continued a couple more blocks before she had him pull up in front of a shabby
hotel. The old red awning hanging in front of the
building was now in tatters.

She waited until he cut the motor off. "Honey,
you want to give me some money so that I can go
in and rent us a room?" she asked quietly. Vickie
opened the front door and got out, not caring
one way or another if the trick spent his money
or not.

"Thank you, darling," Connie said as she took
the money from the hillbilly. She pointed across
the street. "You'll have to turn around and park
over there," she said, "'cause they don't allow no
parkin' in front of the building. Don't worry,
honey," she laughed lightly, "I'll be waitin' for you
in the lobby."

The women moved quickly as the young man
pulled the car away from the curb, making the
tires screech. They walked up the walk leading to
the front door of the hotel, then Connie, leading
the way, cut across the grass, taking the path that

led to the rear of the building. Both girls broke into a run as soon as they got to the side of the building. Again Connie took the lead. She led them down a darkened alley.

Vickie caught herself, to keep from screaming when an alley rat nearly ran across her foot. Connie took her hand and led her slowly as they picked their way through the rubble of a dilapidated barn that should have been torn down. They walked around the side of a house and came out on another street. Crossing over quickly, they again entered another alley. They continued heading west, cutting through yards until both women stopped, completely out of breath. They stood in the backyard of a well-lit house, trying to catch their breath.

Connie pointed at the house. "This is Carl's place, Vickie. If you ain't hip to it, honey, they got an after hours place downstairs in the basement."

"Ohhh, no wonder. I was wondering who stayed here, Connie; just look at all the damn Cadillacs parked in the driveway. Why, it looks like a funeral home or something." Her eyes were large in surprise as she stared around.

Connie laughed lightly. "Come on, girl, we better walk around to the front and find out who's all downstairs before we go barging in."

"How you goin' tell by just going to the front?" Vickie asked naively.

As soon as they reached the front, Connie stopped. "That's how you tell," she said, pointing to Earl's Cadillac parked in front of the house. A little farther down the street, Billy's Caddie could be seen under a streetlamp. She pointed out a forest-green Caddie. "That green one belongs to Carl, the guy who owns this joint." Before she finished speaking, she had spotted the headlights of a car coming down the block. "We better move, damn it. I sure wouldn't want our hillbilly friend to find us this late in the game," she said, then added as they retraced their steps to the back of the yard, "I hope he got smart with some of them guys hanging out at the hotel. They would gladly kick a mudhole in his white ass for him."

Vickie laughed, amused. "There sure is a lot of things I've got to learn yet, isn't there?"

"That's no lie," Connie answered softly. "But it ain't nothing to be ashamed of. Why, as old as I am, I'm still learning things, girl. In the streets, you can learn something different each and every night you're out here, and that ain't no lie." She turned to see if Vickie was listening, then added, "I've been workin' the streets, Vickie, for over seven years now, and something always comes up that's new to me."

"You been workin' for Earl that long, Connie?" Vickie asked her new friend.

"Oh no," Connie answered quickly. "I wish I had, though. I let my high-school boyfriend turn me out, Vickie. I stayed with him for a few years, then one day I ran into Earl."

A cab pulled up in front of the house, cutting

the women's conversation short. "Oh-oh," Connie mumbled. "There's Fay! We better catch that cab, Vickie, and get the hell away from here."

"Why?" Vickie asked sharply. Connie ignored her and yelled at the cab driver.

Fay, a tall, thin, light-complexioned woman with her hair dyed blonde, stepped from the cab. She waved one of her well-manicured hands idly in Connie's direction. "I was under the impression that you were home sick or in the hospital, or something to that effect," Fay said sarcastically, then added, "Looks like I came out to party for nothing, don't it?" Her voice was cold. There was no trace of friendship in it.

Connie ignored her and held the door of the cab open for Vickie. "I make it a point, Vickie, to never become too familiar with sorry whores," she said, loud enough for Fay to overhear. "That way, Vickie, you don't have to worry about none of their sorry-ass ways of whoring rubbing off on you." With that, Connie slammed the cab door, not bothering to speak to Fay.

As the cab pulled away, the heavyset, plump, honey-complexioned woman with Fay put her hands on her hips and asked, "Just who in the hell is *that* supposed to be?" She stared after the disappearing taillights of the car.

Fay's sardonic reply was harsh. "The tall black bitch is just another jealous-hearted whore, Tammy, and you know from experience just how jealous-hearted a black bitch can be, don't you?"

The woman called Tammy shook her head in agreement. "It ain't no dirtier bitch in the world, Fay, than one of those dirty-hearted black bitches," Tammy answered.

Vickie stared out of the back of the cab window; her eyes had never left the face of the woman called Fay, and she couldn't understand so much hatred. She twisted around on the seat and glanced at her friend. Connie wasn't upset at all by the incident. She just settled back in the cab and directed the driver to take them across town.

"We ain't got no time to waste, Vickie, fightin' with no silly-ass bitches. First of all, if we fuck around and cut her yellow ass up, we goin' get in big trouble with Earl, 'cause she's one of his whores. So it don't pay fightin' with her. Second, we don't have to worry about it, 'cause more than likely, when she goes down in the basement and sees Earl, her money ain't goin' be right, not quittin' work this early in the morning. She ain't no thief, so all she can do is fuck, and she ain't fucked up on enough money to make our daddy happy this early in the morning—I'd bet money on that! The bitch is too lazy, so I know her trap ain't right." Connie continued talking as though she were talking to herself. "I'll bet that bitch ends up in trouble before the mornin' is over. All she wants to do is pop her fingers and shake her ass."

"Damn," Vickie exploded angrily. "Just how many goddamn bitches do I have to share Earl with? If she's one of his whores, too, what about that other bitch that was with her? Is she one of our wife-in-laws, too?"

Connie took her time and lit a cigarette before answering. "Fay is the bitch I had to call before we left the apartment this evening. She's the bitch I transferred my dates to. The other bitch, she ain't got nothin' to do with our family." Connie paused and exhaled a cloud of smoke. "Honey, you can't go around being jealous. It just won't do. It makes your life too hard, baby. If you're the jealous type, you should choose a man that ain't got no women at all."

"If she's supposed to be at home taking care of all your dates, Connie, then what's she doing going to the after-hours joint?"

"I don't know, and I don't care, Vickie. It ain't my problem. What I do know is that it ain't goin' make no difference how much money she got, 'cause if she had kept her ass at home, she'd be still making more money, and Earl knows that. She's supposed to stay home and take care of all the phone calls, and if a bitch can't do that, she can't do too much of nothing."

The cab stopped for a red light. Vickie crossed her legs impatiently. "Shit, Connie, how come we didn't go in? We had a good night out in the streets tonight, didn't we?"

Instead of replying, Connie removed a large roll of money from her bra and began to count it. She counted the money quickly, then pushed a hundred and forty dollars into Vickie's hand.

"That was a damn nice sting we took off tonight,
Vickie. It made my trap money sit around two hund-

red and fifty for our troubles tonight."

Vickie removed some money from the top of
her stocking. She put it with that in her lap. "Goddamn, Connie," she said surprised. "I damn near
made three hundred dollars." She counted the
money to make sure.

The cab driver stared at the two women in his
mirror as he pulled up in front of a modern, red
brick house. The neighborhood was well kept.
The people who bought houses in this section of
the city spent money having their lawns and
homes kept in the best of shape.

They paid the driver and got out. Vickie followed Connie into the house. She stared around
at the furnishings in astonishment. "You live here
all by yourself, Connie?"

With a pleased sigh, Connie turned on the living room light. "Just me and my maid, honey. She
takes care of my five-year-old boy, little Tommie."

"Oh, I didn't think you had any children, Connie. You just don't look the type, I guess," Vickie
said as she stared around in open admiration.

"Why? Don't you think I'm old enough to have
them, Vickie?" Connie said sharply.

Vickie blushed. "You know I didn't mean it like
that, Connie. It just didn't occur to me that you
had any children, doing the kind of work you do
and all."

Connie laughed suddenly and broke the slight strain. "Now, Vickie, don't you go and take me wrong. After working with me all night, honey, you should know I ain't got no funny ways by now, girl. Come on, I'll show you where I turn some of my very special tricks."

Without waiting to see if she followed, Connie led off. She went into the kitchen, then opened a door that led down into the basement. Connie hit a wall switch, flooding the basement with light. It revealed a bar and tables arranged around the room. The walls had been paneled in a dark cocoa brown. Connie opened a door and showed her a bedroom. Inside was a beautiful king-sized bed. "I don't never let any of my tricks go upstairs," she said. "This is as far as they get. The basement. There's a toilet over there, and here's the trick room. I've got all the booze they could possibly drink in one lifetime behind the bar, so there ain't no reason for them to go any further in my house."

Connie switched off the lights and led the way back upstairs. "Of course, the only tricks that do get to come out here to my house are the ones that I've been doing business with for years. And it goes without saying that they spend big sums."

"What about your landlord?" Vickie asked quietly. "Or some of your neighbors, for that matter. Don't you worry about them saying something?"

"No problem there. I'm the landlord." Connie

laughed, then added, "After I'd been with Earl for a year, he bought this house for me and my child and put it in my name, honey."

The maid came down the second-floor stairway, interrupting whatever Connie was going to say. The maid had on an old duster, wrapped around her wide frame like a turkish towel. She eyed Vickie sharply, then said, "That goddamn phone's been ringing ever since you left, Connie."

"Well, it ain't my problem. That's Fay's worry now. Don't worry about it, Bertha," Connie replied, then turned to Vickie. "This is a friend of mine. Bertha, this is Vickie. She'll be staying with us for a while, so if you don't mind, Bertha, get the guest room ready for her."

Bertha turned and started back upstairs. "You know damn well the room's already clean, Connie," she muttered. Her voice carried back down to the two women clearly. "Get the guest room ready, huh? Shit." The big woman went on up the steps still mumbling.

Both of the younger women laughed. "Don't pay any attention to her, Vickie. She just wants to mother me—as she'll end up doing to you if you stay here long enough."

The phone rang shrilly. Connie picked up the receiver. She yelled into it, then listened for a few more minutes. She finally agreed, shaking her head as she talked. "Well, it don't look as if we're going to bed any time soon. There's four guys coming over, and each one spends fifty or better."

Connie sat down and crossed her legs. "If it wasn't for that, I would have told them to go straight to hell this morning."

Vickie agreed with her quickly. "At fifty dollars a head, I'll stay up for the rest of the week, honey."

"Good," Connie said, very pleased with her answer. "We better hurry, honey, we got just about enough time to put up our money, change clothes, and grab a quick bath."

As the two young women began to climb the stairs, the phone rang again. Both women continued on up the stairs. Connie pinched Vickie's arm. "It looks as if you and I are going to be two busy little whores this morning."

6

CARL'S AFTER-HOURS JOINT was in full swing when Fay and Tammy entered the fancy basement club. Earl, sitting at the bar, had one arm around Doris and was whispering in her ear when Fay came down the stairs.

Tammy elbowed Fay in the side and pointed at Earl's back. "Ain't that your bigtime pimp over there Fay, spending your money on that funky bitch Doris?"

At the sight of Earl, Fay had hesitated, but Tammy's sharp words goaded her on. Fay was an attractive girl, but one who really wasn't too bright. She loved music and dancing, but other than that she didn't have another thought in her head. She spent all her money on clothes and records.

Just about the same moment, Earl happened to

glance up in the bar mirror, and he didn't like what he saw. He knew Fay was supposed to be working, and the first thing that entered his mind was that something had happened. When she attempted to pass him without speaking, his astonishment turned swiftly to open anger. "Hold on there, bitch," he yelled sharply, then reached out and grabbed her by the arm. "Just where in the fuck do you think you're going?"

"You seemed to be so busy," Fay replied, "I didn't want to disturb you."

Earl removed his arm from around Doris and twisted on his stool so that he was facing Fay. "I didn't ask you, bitch, about what I was doing! I asked about what the fuck you were doing here."

The people near them at the bar and nearest tables suddenly became silent. Fay tossed her head back, making the long blonde wig fall across her shoulders. She stared around at the people watching before replying. "I could ask *you* the same thing, Earl," she flipped, then raising her voice added, "but then I don't have to ask; all I have to do is look."

Before the words were out of her mouth, Earl had slipped from the stool. He slapped her viciously across the mouth. Before he could slap her again, Carl, the owner of the bar, stepped between them.

"Temper, temper," Carl said lightly, placing his hand on Earl's shoulder. "Take her upstairs or, better yet, Earl, out in the alley. But please, man, respect my place. I can't stand no kind of rumbles in here."

Earl was a tall man himself, but he still had to look up at the smiling man who had his hand on his shoulder. Earl glared at Fay over Carl's shoulder. He couldn't really think straight because of what the woman had said. It had been a long time since a woman had had the nerve to sass him that much. Right then, all he could imagine was putting his foot in Fay's ass. Carl's words didn't even ring a bell with him. Without even thinking, Earl attempted to step around Carl.

"Wait a minute, my man," Carl said quickly, pushing him back slightly.

There it was. It was out in the open. Doris slid off her stool quickly. "You ain't got no reason to put your hands on him," she screamed at Carl as she rushed up beside Earl. Carl stepped back, surprised.

He spoke up quickly to Earl. "Man, how about keeping your crazy-ass women out of this. I don't want no problems, Earl, you know that, man."

Doris broke a beer bottle. "Don't make the mistake and push him again," she screamed, waving the broken glass in the air.

"Well, I'll be goddamned," Carl exclaimed. He stepped back out of reach. "Man, please take your crazy-ass bitches out of here, please Earl?" he pleaded, all the while watching Doris out of the corner of his eye. His bouncers ran up. Carl waved them away. "Look here, man, just leave, please. I'll take care of your bar bill, so don't worry about nothing. When everything's together, the joint will still be here."

Earl pointed at Fay. "Come on, bitch, I want to see you outside."

"I ain't going nowhere!" Fay answered loudly, shaking her head all the time. "Not me, baby. I ain't going out the door."

Carl interrupted. "That's bullshit, girl. You goin' take your ass out of here, and right now." He nodded his head, and one of his doormen rushed over and grabbed her arm. Another one grabbed her from behind and both the men rushed her towards the door as she screamed.

"Damn, Earl, I'm sorry about this," Carl said apologetically. "You know you and me ain't never had no misunderstanding, so I hope this little thing don't mean nothing, my man."

"Don't worry about it, Carl, this was all my fault," Earl replied easily, then added, "besides, my man, when did we ever let a funky bitch come between two men, huh?" Earl laughed quietly, then turned on his heel and started for the door before Carl could even reply. Carl let out a sigh of relief as he watched Doris follow her man out the door. Silently, he promised himself to repay Doris for her act of hostility. It would be a long time before he forgot that she had broken a beer bottle with the intention of doing him bodily harm. Yes, he thought coldly, it would be a hell of a long time before he forgot her little act of violence.

As the doorman let Fay out, he spoke over his shoulder to Earl. "Why don't you take her down the street, my man? Our neighbors have been complaining enough already without them having a heavyweight fight on their front lawn."

Earl ignored the bouncer's remark and grabbed Fay's arm before she could run. "Don't worry," he yelled to the doorman. "I'm going to give Carl's place the same respect I'd give my mother's house."

Fay spoke up suddenly. The whiskey she had drunk earlier had worn off. "I didn't see you slapping Connie's goddamn face when she left out of here, Earl."

Not really understanding what she meant, Earl grabbed her by both arms and shook her viciously. He released one of her arms and slapped her across the mouth. "Don't you worry about Connie, bitch! Wherever she's at, you can bet business is being taken care of."

"Was the bitch takin' care of business when she was down in Carl's joint a few minutes ago?" Her voice was full of hostility as she screamed in his face.

Earl slapped her again, then pushed her towards the car. "No good, funky-ass bitch! Shut your lying ass mouth. That's just about all you're good for, Fay, is lying, or to start some bullshit. I've been downstairs for the past two hours, bitch, and Connie ain't been nowhere near the place tonight." His anger grew as he yelled at her, and with one violent motion, he knocked her on the ground.

Fay was sobbing deeply and loudly as she picked herself up from the grass. She wiped her mouth as a tiny trickle of blood ran down her chin. Doris ran around in front of her and opened the car door. Earl snatched her towards him, then shoved her against the car. She scrambled towards the door. He kicked her brutally as she tried to jump into the open car door.

"Get the hell over," Doris snarled at Fay as she climbed into the car beside the frightened woman. Fay, finding herself wedged in between Doris and Earl, began to cry and plead loudly. All of the nerve she had had earlier had disappeared. "Please, Earl," she cried, "I ain't did nothing, daddy. Nothing at all. I didn't mean no harm, honey, I swear I didn't."

"I should kill you, bitch," Earl said harshly. "Never in my life have I had a bitch disrespect me the way you did tonight, whore!"

"Oh, Earl, honey, please listen, baby. I didn't mean no harm, daddy. I just got mad after seeing Connie and that other girl leaving out of here, Earl, and I had dropped some red devils earlier tonight. So baby, I just got beside myself. But I'm truly sorry, daddy. I really mean it. I been home all night taking care of Connie's tricks while she was down here poppin'. You know that made me mad, daddy."

Trying to hold his anger from reaching the boiling point, Earl asked sharply, "I don't think nothing is wrong with your eyesight, Doris, so will you tell this dizzy-ass bitch whether or not you saw Connie downstairs tonight?"

"I ain't seen Connie in over a month, Fay, and I've been downstairs with Earl all night. She sure in the fuck ain't been in there in the last three hours, and you can take that for real, honey, 'cause I ain't got no reason to lie about it, no reason whatsoever."

The sound of an open palm across Fay's cheekbone split the night air. "Lie to me one more time tonight, bitch, and I'll pull you out of this car and break both your motherfuckin' legs! Do I make myself clear?" His voice shook as he tried to control the anger that was building up in him.

Fay stared from Earl to Doris. She didn't know what to say. Beyond a shadow of a doubt, she knew she had seen Connie, but she knew better than to mention it again. She quickly decided to change the subject. "Well, anyway, daddy, I took care of your business. I made your money right before I left the pad, baby, and I left the money home so that there wouldn't be any chance of me messing it up."

"How much?" he inquired sharply. There was not a trace of a smile on his cold features as he waited for her answer.

"Uh . . . , uh, I got," she stuttered as she attempted to answer, "I got close to a hundred dollars put up for you, honey."

He pulled to the curb quickly. Before she could react, his hand shot out and he slapped her viciously across the face. "Whore! No-good-ass bitch! Funky bitch! Don't you realize that it's been over three days since the last time I've seen you? No-good-ass whore! You mean to sit there and tell me that that's all the money you got?" Earl shook his head as if a sharp pain had hit him in the head. He backhanded her across the mouth. He grabbed her hair with one hand and slapped her face with the other.

"Oh, God, please, someone help me!" she begged, as tears ran down her cheeks and mingled with the blood running from her mouth and nose. "Please, daddy, please. I'll go to work right now if it will make you happy," she begged.

Doris turned her face away, not wanting to watch what was happening beside her. It was Fay's own fault, she reasoned harshly.

"Please, Earl, please! Just let me out of the car, daddy, and tell me how much money you want me to make. I won't bother to go to sleep until I've got your money right, Earl. I mean it, daddy. Just give me another chance. I'll take care of business, daddy."

Earl stared at her coldly. Without answering, he slipped the Caddie into gear and pulled away from the curb. The big car floated out into the morning darkness. The stars still glittered brightly above them, but there was a slight tint in the sky, warning of the coming dawn.

Doris removed some tissue from a box under the seat. "You better wipe your face, Fay, before you get blood all over the car, girl." There was no tenderness in her voice. She gave the impression that she was more concerned with the car than with her wife-in-law's well-being. Generally, no matter how cold hearted a prostitute became, she could usually find some kind of compassion in her heart for a working companion, but in this case, there was none. Doris realized that she could have been on the receiving end just as well as Fay, but it didn't disturb her at all. It was Fay's problem, and as far as Doris was concerned, she had brought the whole damn thing down on her own head.

Fay took the tissue and cleaned her face. Between sobs she managed to ask, "Just tell me, Earl, what do you want me to do?"

He took his eyes from the road for a moment. "Nothing, bitch, nothing at all. You done did all you're ever going to do for me in this lifetime, bitch."

It took a minute for his words to really dawn on her. "What, baby? What you mean by that?" she asked, hurt. She still couldn't believe what she had heard.

"You know what I mean, bitch!" he answered harshly. "As soon as we get to the apartment and I get to tossing your goddamn clothes out, you'll really get the message," he added.

She was struck dumbfounded. She had known what he had meant from the first, but her mind wouldn't accept it for what it was. "Please, baby," she pleaded, and now there was a sound of urgency in her voice. "Don't put me out, daddy. Don't do that to me, honey. Whatever I did that you think was wrong, it couldn't be that bad."

Fay lost her voice for a moment, then continued. "I don't care if you beat me with an ironing cord, Earl, but please don't put me out, honey. Don't do that to me. No, God, no. Don't make me leave you, honey. Don't do that to me."

His voice was so cold when he answered that he even frightened Doris. "You're going, bitch, out of my life. And I don't mean next week sometime—tonight, whore, this very goddamn night! And I'm goin' make sure you're packed so that you'll have no reason to ever come back."

"What, baby?" she asked, hurt, knowing what he said but still not wanting to accept it. "What, daddy? What you mean by that? I know I ain't did nothing to deserve you treatin' me like that." She stared at him, and now the tears really did flow down her cheeks. "Earl, baby, you know I ain't never wanted nobody but you, honey, so don't say them mean words to me, please." There was a deep earnestness in her voice, and her eyes were horror stricken. "I don't care if you beat me every day this week, daddy, just don't make me leave you. Don't do that to me." There was a danger signal in her words, but he paid no heed to them.

"Don't beg, bitch, 'cause it ain't goin' do you no good," he stated as he reached over and twisted the knob on the radio, searching for a jazz station.

STREET PLAYERS

There was a stillness in the car. Doris felt it. She glanced at the other occupants. She had listened quietly to the argument, measuring his every word. She had just chosen Earl, in fact, earlier in the evening. She had given him some money that she had been saving for over a week so that her trap money would be right when she came to him. She detested a violent pimp, and from her knowledge, Earl was not one of those kind who liked to beat up his women. Even though he had slapped Fay tonight, she could tell he was not a real violent man. Some of the men she had known in the past would have strumped Fay for the way she had acted earlier. From what she had seen, she believed that Fay was getting off light for the way she had acted. True enough, it hurt to be fired by a pimp, because all of the other girls would be talking about it. But she honestly believed that Fay had brought the whole thing on herself. Some pimps were notorious for their brutality, but Earl had just the opposite reputation. Oh well, she reasoned, if Fay hadn't disrespected him so in front of all the other pimps and hustlers, she probably would have gotten off a whole lot easier. Any woman should know she couldn't get away with screaming on her man in front of a bar full of players. If he was any kind of man at all, he'd have to do something to regain his pride.

Earl pulled up and parked in front of a modern three-story building on the less fashionable section of the east side. His voice was harsh as he spoke to Fay. "Wipe some of that damn blood off your face, woman, or go around to the alley and come in the back door."

There was still quite a bit of blood on her face. Doris held out some more tissue for her. As she climbed out of the car, Doris waited and wiped some blood from Fay's neck. Between them, they were able to get her face clean enough to be passable.

"That's better," Doris said lightly. "You might not be able to pass any beauty contests, hon, but at least the police won't stop us because of your appearance."

The elevator hummed softly as it lifted them slowly up to the third floor. They got out and waited patiently until Fay had opened the door to the large two-bedroom apartment.

"My, my, my," Doris said excitedly. "I'd never have thought from the outside that they had such lovely apartments in this building." She stared around in amazement. The wall-to-wall carpet was a loud pink, with deep black throw rugs criss-crossing the floor. The furniture was a matching black velvet couch with a large love seat that must have cost over five hundred dollars for the chair alone. The place looked like money. It was the most beautiful place Doris had ever seen in her life. It would be a thrill just to live here, she thought.

"You won't find no other apartments in this building like this one," Earl stated flatly. "I had that bar," he said, pointing at the bar covering the whole northern wall, "built just to my own specifications. The size, color—everything—I ordered specifically. I had a crew of carpenters come up here and build it right on that goddamn spot." There was the sound of pride in his voice. He twisted around and pointed to the drapes. "Them we picked up in Los Angeles and shipped back here. That's over five hundred dollars worth of drapery."

Noticing the change in his mood, Fay spoke up. "The rent for the place don't run but one hundred and fifty a month, Doris. You can't hardly find a place this nice nowhere for that price."

Earl glared at Fay and nodded towards the bedroom. "Well, that's one thing you won't have to worry about no more, bitch. Now get your lazy ass in there and pack your goddamn clothes before I get mad and toss all the motherfuckin' things you own out the goddamn nearest window."

For one brief second, Doris felt a pang of pity for Fay. She attempted to speak up. "Earl. . . ."

"Earl, my ass, bitch!" Fay screamed, interrupting her. "If it wasn't for you, whore, wouldn't none of this shit have happened. One of you no-good bitches are always trying to get in somebody else's game, you dirty, black-ass bitch, you!" Fay cursed angrily as tears ran down her cheeks.

With an unusual show of control, Doris held her temper. She realized Fay was deeply hurt. It was very seldom that a pimp fired a good whore.

Usually it was the other way around. A good prostitute could just about choose any man she wanted who was in the life. A good prostitute was always in demand. Doris turned away as Fay went into a crying fit. It was not a convulsive outburst, it was sheer weeping, without a sob in it. It was a grief, a release from rigidity, vast and inconsolable, as Fay realized that she had really blown her man.

She turned on Doris with the fury of a tiger. "That's all you do is hang around on bar stools meddling everybody's man but your own, bitch!" she cried out, her pride hurt more than anything else.

Without saying a word, Earl walked over to Fay and knocked her down. The blow was hard and straight to her jaw. She crumpled up as though struck by lightning. She fell to his feet, and he kicked her viciously in the head, twice. Then he reached down and pulled her back to her feet and knocked her down again. She cried out in pain.

"Please, please, please, I'm leaving! Don't hit me no more. I'll leave, Earl, I'll leave. Just don't hurt me. Please don't hurt me!"

Earl stared down at her for a moment. "I done told you what to do, hard-headed-ass bitch! Now ain't I? Don't make me have to repeat myself again, Fay, 'cause it ain't goin' hurt nobody but you. You understand me, girl?"

"I'm going, I'm going," Fay cried as she crawled towards the bedroom, afraid to climb to her feet.

In less than ten minutes, Fay emerged from the bedroom lugging two suitcases and carrying a small color television under her arm. "I'll send somebody else around later on today to pick up the rest of my stuff, Earl," she said as she sniffed, trying to hold back a sob. She set one bag down, opened the door, and fought back the tears as she spoke to Earl. "Ain't no nigger, red or black, Earl, ever kicked me before," she said. Sparks of hate glittered in her greenish eyes.

Doris shivered slightly at the sight of so much unleashed hatred, but Earl ignored her anger and said, as he started towards her, "I'll bet ain't no nigger ever kicked you down three flights of stairs, either, whore, but if you open your funky mouth again, I'm going to make that a first, too."

She slammed the door behind her before he could reach it, dragging her bags and staggering towards the elevator. She went through the lobby carrying her bags and crying openly. The few people up who witnessed her embarrassment turned their faces so that they wouldn't have to see her shame.

Fay ran into the middle of the street and stopped the first cab she saw. Jumping in, she said, "Take me to the nearest police station."

7

AFTER MAKING ARRANGEMENTS to have Doris's clothes picked up and brought over to her new apartment, Earl departed. It had been difficult convincing her that the flat had never really belonged to Fay, and now Earl smiled as he remembered their brief argument. She really hadn't believed him until he told her that her stay there would be of short duration, because the steady business that came to the apartment demanded a steady supply of different girls. As Earl climbed into his car, he could feel the heat from a brassy sun that hung furnace hot, seemingly motionless. And even as it made its flaming dip toward the horizon, the heat remained, reflected from the dirty gray walls of the crumbling tenements that he drove past.

Earl glanced at his watch; it was close to nine.

If he rushed, he could catch his brother before he went off to work and have breakfast with him. He stopped his car and made a call so that his food would be ready by the time he got there. Back in the car, he reflected on the trouble he had had that morning. He disliked brutality in any form, but he carried no delusions about its use—especially when dealing with whores. In his profession, it became a necessity to resort to violence at times. He tried to honestly analyze his acts, reprimanding himself harshly for losing his temper and allowing his anger to overcome his reason. The hell with it, he thought, I'd rather hurt my foot on a hardheaded bitch's head than hurt my hand. He believed this with full male conceit.

As he pulled off the freeway, he couldn't help but notice all the new construction work going on. He made a right turn and drove towards Conant Gardens. In another five minutes, he passed a large sign stating that he had entered Blossom Estates, a new inter racial suburb that hadn't been completed yet. Empty half-finished houses sat on lots with large piles of sand in front of them.

Earl noticed a large home that had just been completed. A sign stating "Shimashi and Jones Contractors" sat on the dark green lawn. With a slight smile he remembered the sharp Japanese and Negro businessmen. By smart connections, they had made financial arrangements so that they had the complete gigantic job of building all the homes in the suburb. Earl had wanted to invest some money in the project with them, but they had refused.

He pulled up and parked in front of the house he had put a downpayment on for his mother. The large backyard had been planned when he had the house built. He had wanted a swimming pool, but his sister-in-law had rejected his women so coldly when he brought them around that he had decided to not waste any money for a pool he couldn't use.

He realized that his brother and his wife were plotting so that they could end up with the house, but it didn't really disturb him. When he had agreed to help buy the house, Eddie and his pious wife had tried to take over the house hunting, so he had gone out and spent big money to have one built. Not really caring if they liked the house or not, he could have always moved in if nobody else wanted it.

Eddie's wife, Jan, had had a fit. Earl laughed as he thought about the way she had carried on. The veins in her fat neck had bulged as she blurted, "Oh no, that wouldn't do at all. Why, if we left it up to you, you'd more than likely have one built down there in those slums where you hang out." Eddie had laughed on cue, but after the laughter Earl had gone right on and had a house built anyway, without their okay.

When Jan had seen the house completed, she had remarked dryly, "Just what Mother needs, a two-car garage, and she doesn't even drive. And the lawn is so large it will take her at least two weeks to cut the grass." She had twisted her nose up, then added, "I don't see why you bothered to have four bedrooms. That's way too many."

"The bedrooms are for whenever Eddie or I decide to visit," Earl had said. "We're not in the habit of sharing the same bed with our mother, you know." Earl didn't miss the sly glance that went between the couple.

Eddie had spoken up without a quaver. "I thought I had told you, Earl, uh, me and Jan had decided to move in with Mother. Since we're going to pay half the house notes, we might as well cut down on some of our overhead, too."

"There's no reason to let her live by herself," Jan quickly said, adding her contribution. "Your mother is getting up in age, boy, and you ain't goin' take the time from your whoring to look after her."

Earl had stared from one to the other. After that, he had never really cared for the house. It didn't make any difference to him about his brother staying at the house, but the slyness of the couple in trying to get him to pay half of everything was sickening. He could well afford it, so the money didn't bother him like it worried Eddie and Jan. But he knew as well as the slick couple that the house was really theirs. He had started to put the house in his name only, but Jan had really carried on. Her face had turned gray and her big owlish eyes had almost popped through the thick glasses she wore.

Climbing out of his car, Earl's smile disap- peared as he remembered Jan's sharp words that day. "In *your* name!" she had screamed bitterly. "Why? So you can come along one day with one of those tramp women you keep and put all of us out? No way, baby, no way!"

Eddie, knowing Earl quite well, spoke up quickly. "Besides, Earl," he added hurriedly, dropping his arm around Earl's shoulder to stop him if he should decide to drop a punch on Jan, "you'd probably have trouble getting it in your name anyway. You ain't never worked nowhere, baby brother."

Jan was not accustomed to contradiction, and she was naive enough to believe everything should go her way whenever she asserted her foolish opinion. Her voice was full of malice when she spoke. "Eddie, I don't care who might not like it, but I've got just as much say-so as anybody else."

Eddie had been nagged and henpecked by Jan since marriage, as Earl well knew. This was the first time the woman had directed her sharp tongue in Earl's direction, and he didn't like it. He had never liked the dominating woman because of the way she treated his brother, but since he didn't have to put up with it, he never stepped between them; he held too much pride to allow the woman to administer a tongue-lashing at him, however, so he spoke directly to her. "Just shut up! I don't give a damn what you and Eddie do. Ya'll ain't got to do nothing; I'll buy the house for Mom myself, and ya'll buy your own goddamn house."

Eddie was shocked. He knew he and Jan didn't have enough money between them to get the kind of house he could get from Earl. He sturnbled towards a chair and sat down dumbfounded. It took a few seconds for Earl's words to sink into Jan's mind. When they did and the meaning was clear, she was bewildered. She hadn't meant for him to take that attitude. She knew it was no idle boast that he would buy the house alone for his mother. If that were to happen, she felt she would never get the opportunity to own a house as luxurious as the one Earl would get. In her mind, she could picture the house drifting farther and farther away. A lump came to her throat, and she prayed that she wouldn't start crying. She cursed under her breath and wondered if she would always have to live in a Negro-infested neighborhood. She had prayed and hoped and dreamed and planned until her dream had almost come true. She remembered when she had first gotten the idea, and how clever she had been in making Eddie think it was *his* idea. It was even her idea to involve Earl in the financial aspects of the deal. She had known there were nice interracial neighborhoods where the homes cost so much that only a very few blacks could really afford to live there. "What about your mother, Earl?" she asked desperately. "Isn't there some way we could put *her* name on the deed?"

With the innocence of elderly people, his mother spoke up. "That sounds all right to me, son. Anything to stop the fussing."

Earl, still angry, said loudly. "I'll have one built for you, Mom, without the help of anyone. It don't make a damn bit of difference to me, one way or another. I don't need their goddamn money to do nothing."

"Now don't cuss, Earl. That ain't right—you know better than that," his mother said. "Whatever we do, let's do it without a lot of fuss, 'cause I can always stay where I'm at."

That cooled both of the brothers down, then Eddie found his voice at last and said, "It won't be necessary, Earl, for you to do that. If we go ahead like we planned, it will be cheaper for both of us."

Before Earl had driven them home, Jan had apologized a dozen times. She had lost a lot of points in his book that day, he remembered as he walked up the path. Whenever he visited, she never missed an opportunity to needle him for rubbing her face in shit that day and making her chew it with a smile.

Earl's mother opened the door for him and he kissed her on the cheek. He held her at arm's length. "Mom, you done got fat as hell since the last time I was out here."

"My sugar's all right, Earl. I ain't been eatin'

STREET PLAYERS

much junk, so it ain't no problem." She laughed lightly as she hugged her youngest son. She was a round woman with graying hair and a fat face. Her eyes glittered like marbles as she stared up, admiring her son with affection. "Come on in the kitchen, son," she said. "I've got your grits ready, with your eggs, just like you like them."

Earl kidded her as he walked into the kitchen. "Ain't you niggers learned yet that with all this room you ain't supposed to eat in the servant's quarters? Why, what would your white neighbors think of you if they was to catch you doing that?"

"That's what I always tell them, Earl," Jan said from the other side of the small table. Jan had gained some weight and she appeared to be larger than Earl remembered. It had been a few months since he had come out to visit. The smile he had held for his mother disappeared as he turned to Jan. He silently wished he had never joked about the kitchen now after finding Jan taking his point of view. He didn't want to agree with his sister-in-law on anything. He realized instantly that she hadn't realized he had been joking with his mother, and she would end up using his little remark to gain her way another day when he wasn't there, to get her will obeyed by his mother and her husband.

"Well," his mother said good-naturedly, "I ain't never seen nothing wrong with eating here, but Jan's always complaining. And with you knowing about such things, Earl, if you said it ain't right, I guess it ain't. An old fool like me don't know nothing no way."

With his eyes gleaming, Earl walked over and hugged his mother tightly. "Woman, whenever I come over and eat, I don't want to be served anywhere else but in the kitchen."

His mother grinned widely. "I always knowed you was nothing but a big country boy underneath," she said.

During the meal, Earl found out that Jan was not going to work that day, so Earl made his exit when Eddie was leaving for work. He and his brother had hardly spoken since his arrival, still, Earl waved cheerfully at his brother from the driveway. He backed the big Cadillac out into the street. His mother stood out on the porch watching him, so he blew her a kiss. He watched in his mirror and saw her stand on the porch until he was just about out of sight. He wondered sadly if she was really happy in that house with her daughter-in-law. He made a mental note that he would find out about it in the near future, not realizing that his own problems would get so big that he wouldn't have time for his mother's.

8

EARL TOOK HIS TIME driving, but he finally reached Twelfth Street and parked in front of the Chicken Shack. The Chicken Shack was a small restaurant that many of the nightlife crowd picked to patronize because it stayed open twenty-four hours and served good food. Earl pushed the door open and stared around at the people who refused to submit to nature's urging their tired bodies to go home. They gathered together in the mornings from the sleepless wanderings of the night before—either to gamble, gossip, or try to steal a friend's woman. There was a crowd of teenage boys loitering near the door who had either managed to get up early or to stay out all night without their parents' consent. They yelled, calling Earl by his nickname, "the Black Pearl," and when he spoke to them, they all grinned happily because a pimp of his status had bothered to speak.

Earl knew that the young boys could stay on the fringe of big money until they broke apart from each other, for each had a separate path to follow. Some of them would find the penitentiary waiting down the road for them with open gates, while some of the other ones might get lucky and get a good whore. That would keep them out of jail for a while.

Against the walls, sitting in the booths, were the prostitutes who hadn't made their nightly quotas. Each time the door opened, they smiled brightly, only to turn back sulkingly over their stale cups of coffee. Charles yelled from a booth he was occupying with two ladies of the night. He grinned broadly and beckoned for Earl to join them. "I hear you put on a main event last night, baby. That don't sound like you," he said, flashing his teeth and laughing all the while.

Earl's cantankerous mood seemed to dissolve as he slid smoothly into the booth. "Well, Charles," he said lightly, "you know how that thing goes. Any man would like to always rule by the *right*, but sometimes you're forced to rule by *might.*" Earl turned to the blonde girl next to him. "What's been happening, Pat? I thought you and Billy had hooked up for the day."

She pretended to be irked by the remark.

"What kind of whore do you think I am? I don't sleep with no man that ain't spending money with me, unless it's my man."

Charles stopped from biting his nails long enough to remark dryly, "Bitch, you ain't got nothing better to do than sit over there and tell them goddamn lies?" Before she could reply, he continued, speaking to Earl. "Some new, white, redheaded bitch come through here this morning, and when Billy pulled up from here with her Pat damn near had a fit."

Earl laughed coldly. "Everywhere I went last night I run into them, Charles. They were all wrapped up like honeymooners. Now, you know I know Pat been after Billy and his bag for the longest—since he's supposed to have the best poison in town."

Tammy punched Charles in the ribs with her elbow. "What kind of poison does he have?" she asked curiously.

Earl stared across the table at Tammy. More to change the subject than any other reason, he asked, "Didn't I see you with Fay last night?"

Tammy laughed nervously. "Yes, I was with her for a while, but you took her out of that after-hours place and left me all by my lonesome."

Earl stared at the plump woman. "I'd guess from that statement that you ain't got no man, either?" he asked quickly.

Charles pulled the woman towards him. "She

got somebody now," he said, hugging Tammy tightly. His dark eyes glittered with excitement as he continued, "She done chose her a real pimp, Earl. She ain't got one of them niggers out here shortstopping."

For a brief moment, Earl had to turn his face away so that he didn't laugh at his partner then he stated, "If it was left up to you, Pat, she'd end up spending all her goddamn money on stuff. Bitch, that's all you do with yours."

Tammy was a fat-faced woman with large cheekbones. She stared around stupidly. "What is he talking about now, Charles? Stuff? What kind of stuff?"

Before he could answer, two well-dressed white men entered the restaurant. They stopped in the doorway and stared around. Most of the prostitutes sitting around the restaurant stared back with plenty of hostility, as only the most inexperienced whore couldn't recognize the men for police. Their eyes searched each booth, returning stare for stare, without blinking. The gray-haired officer touched his partner's arm and nodded towards Earl's table.

"Oh damn," Pat moaned, "here comes the fuckin' fuzz straight to our table."

Earl spoke up sharply. "Just don't push no dope up under this table, bitch. I ain't for handling no funny case because of you, whore!"

Pat ignored Earl. Her hands moved under the

table and a small package slipped out of her hand onto the floor. She took her foot and pushed it over between Tammy's feet.

The officers stopped at the table. "Earl Williams," the gray-headed one said dryly, "you're under arrest."

Earl stared up at the two men, stunned. "For what?" he managed to ask.

The youngest one of the two officers removed a warrant from his pocket. "For pandering, pimp. Let's go," he said, reaching down and pulling Earl to his feet. Astonishment was Earl's first reaction, but as the police pushed him out of the door, anger replaced his shock.

"What the fuck . . . ," he started to say, but was interrupted by the young officer. "I told you to be quiet, boy; now don't make me repeat myself."

Earl ignored the officer and turned to Charles, who had followed them out of the restaurant. "Call Connie, Charles, and have her reach my lawyer for me," he said.

The young officer turned and slapped Earl viciously across the mouth. "I told you to shut your fuckin' mouth, nigger!"

Before Earl could react, the older officer stepped between them. He pushed Earl into the back of the car and cautioned, "Just do like you're told and nothing will happen. But start some shit and you'll lose every goddamn thing."

Earl glared from the backseat at the younger officer. "If that cocksucker puts his hands on me again, something goin' happen to one of us," he said angrily.

As the older officer walked around the car to get in on the driver's side, the young one turned in his seat. "You lowlife bastard," he said, "you. . . ." He didn't get a chance to complete his statement. Earl hit him between the eyes, and before the young officer could retaliate, he hit him again. Earl became a black streak, throwing punches from the shoulder. The officer who was struck managed to open the door, but as he staggered out, Earl jumped from the backseat and buffeted him with a barrage of punches until the officer slumped to the curb.

A warning was sounded from the crowd, but before Earl could spin around, the older officer hit him from behind with his blackjack, and Earl slipped quietly to the sidewalk.

A passing cruiser pulled over and two uniformed officers jumped out with their guns drawn. It didn't take a minute for them to disperse the crowd.

Charles had watched the brief fight from the protection of the entrance to the restaurant. After the arrival of more policemen, he quickly entered the restaurant and walked back towards the booth they had just vacated. He stopped and retraced his steps, heading towards the pay telephone.

Connie's maid answered the telephone, causing him to wait impatiently while she went to awaken Connie. From the phone booth, Charles watched closely as Pat retrieved her package of dope from the side of the table Charles had been occupying. The sound of Connie's voice on the other end of the line stopped him from leaving the phone booth immediately.

He closed the phone booth door. "Connie? I got some bad news for you, girl. This is Charles, baby. Now listen, and stop asking crazy-ass questions. The Man done busted Earl. That's right, they just picked him up. The Man said something about a pandering case. He had a warrant, too."

All the traces of sleep that had been in her voice earlier were gone now. "There must be some kind of mistake, Charles. You know as well as I that Earl don't do nothing wrong."

Like most bearers of sad tidings, Charles seemed to prolong the tension. It appeared that he enjoyed the role that was pushed on him. "What you mean, girl? Nothing wrong! He ain't got no license to pimp, plus he kicked the shit out of one of the police officers."

"What?" she exclaimed. "This shit don't sound right at all Charles, you ain't been drinkin' or something, have you? I mean, you wouldn't be playing no joke on me or something like that? It don't even sound right. Earl? Fightin' the police?"

"Connie, you know me better than that. Ain't no way in the fuckin' world would I play with you about something like this. Besides, Earl told me to tell you to get on the case as soon as possible."

Connie became silent for a moment. "Well, I'd better get our lawyer on the case then." Her next words were spoken more to herself than Charles. "If I call him now, I stand a good chance of catching him at home before he goes to the office." She hesitated, then said, "Thanks for calling, Charles. I'll get right on it. It's hard to believe, but I'm sure you ain't bullshittin'. That fightin' against the police is really hard to believe. If you're lying, it's your ass, not mine. Well, anyway, I'm going on and call the lawyer." She waited, hoping that Charles would tell her to stop, that it was all a game between Earl and Charles. She held her breath, hoping that Earl would get on the phone, but when nothing happened, she slowly hung the phone up, then began dialing the high-priced lawyer.

9

IN THE OPINION of the underworld characters who were supposed to be in the know, Earl's young, blond headed lawyer was believed to be the best in the city. At the moment, his sharp features were cast in the red hue of anger. He pushed his glasses higher on the bridge of his long Jewish nose and glared at the desk sergeant.

He wasn't the only one who was angry. The desk sergeant's face looked like a ripe tomato as he listened to the young attorney's sharp words. He shouldn't have felt too bad because many an opposing attorney had gotten red around the ears after listening to Milton Mills' shrewd summation in court.

The desk sergeant's anger didn't disturb Attorney Mills at all. "Now, Sergeant, I don't have all day to wait for you to make up your mind to release my client. I've been trying to explain it to you, sir, that you have nothing else more important than the job of releasing my client." The lawyer removed a small form from his pocket. "I have a writ here from Judge Rubenstein ordering that my client be released in my custody until we appear in his courtroom this afternoon."

The desk sergeant raised his hands in the air. "I understand. As I said earlier, we're going to release him, but the detectives want to talk to him first."

The attorney laughed, but there was no humor in his voice. "Now, Sergeant, I don't know how naive you think I am, but I'm well aware of the fight my client was supposed to have had with one of your detectives, so I'd think they would like to keep him around for more than just a few hours. But, as I've stated, I don't have the time and, in fact, I've wasted more time than I can afford discussing this matter with you. Now, would you please trot on back there and get my client, or do I have to inform the judge that you wouldn't acknowledge his writ?"

The other police officers standing around attempted to act as though they weren't listening, but their silence gave them away. Any other time, they would have been horseplaying with each other, but now they were all ears.

"All right, young man, I'll see what I can do. But you understand I'm just following orders myself," the sergeant stated as he picked up the desk phone and spoke quietly into it. A bellow came back over the receiver, and Mills could make out every word the turnkey said.

"What the hell," the turnkey screamed on the other end of the line. "Them detectives are going to be mad as hell. They really wanted us to hold onto this punk. But if you say so, I'll bring the punk out."

"Do it then, damn it, and without so damn much mouth," the desk sergeant stated, his anger slowly rising.

In the rear of the police station, the turnkey stopped in front of Earl's cell. He took his keys and rapped on the bars. "Get your ass up, big shot. Looks like somebody took an interest in your ass."

Earl stood up and stretched. The tiny cell was just that—tiny. It had a face bowl but no toilet. Instead of a bunk or bed, there was an iron slab hanging from the wall. Earl had been using his shoes for a pillow. He reached down and hurriedly put them on. The quicker he got out of the funky place, the better he'd feel.

"Come on," the turnkey growled, even though he saw that Earl was hurrying. "You keep poking around, boy, and I'll lock the fuckin' door back up!"

Earl glared at the turnkey. His calling Earl "boy" made him mad as hell, but he knew that if he let them know they got under his skin with such jive, they'd only run it in the ground. He took his time and tossed some water in his face so that he could get the sleep out of his eyes. He tried to pat his natural so that it wouldn't look too bad, then followed the hostile guard through the doors until he was in front of his lawyer and the desk sergeant. The other policemen stared at him hotly. The word of his fight with the detective had spread, and now all of the uniformed officers were trying to remember his face so that they could get him whenever they saw him in the streets. Earl could tell from the stares that, whenever one of them got a chance, he would end up getting a ticket or being brought down to the station on suspicion of something. They could hold him seventy-two hours on a suspicion charge if he didn't have the money to get a writ.

He followed his attorney out of the police station and over to the courtroom. It seemed as though they had just entered when Earl heard his name called. The judge was a small, shriveled old man. He examined Earl with a cold detachment that left Earl feeling weird. As the judge studied some papers in front of him, Earl glanced around and saw Connie in the back of the courtroom. He smiled to himself. He knew she had been there all day, more than likely, trying to get him free.

The judge spoke up, asking Earl how he was going to plead. His attorney put in his "not guilty" plea. The judge hesitated briefly, then set bond at ten thousand dollars. Earl's attorney almost went through the roof of the courtroom. The judge got mad.

STREET PLAYERS

"From what these papers say," the judge said sternly, "I'd think the young man got off lightly. I don't have any pity for a man who fights with arresting officers—not to mention what he is charged with." The judge stared down at them. "Yes, I'd say this young man is getting off very lightly."

Connie listened quietly from the back of the courtroom. When she heard the bond, she turned to the handsome, well-dressed Jewish bondsman sitting next to her. "Here, Sam, you might as well get your money now. I don't quite have that much. That bastard! You know ten thousand dollars is too fuckin' much."

Sam grinned down at the tall, dark-complexioned girl next to him. He had been doing business with them for years, and he had a lot of respect for Connie. They had a close familiarity that only a long acquaintance could bring. "I don't worry about the money with you or Earl, Connie. But I do believe it was extra high. I guess the judge is kind of hoping your old man can't make it." He laughed, then added, "I'd have sprung him if you didn't have a penny—so up the old bastard's ass."

Both of them laughed as she slipped five hundred dollars into his hand. Sam put the money into his inside pocket without even counting it. Now that she knew Earl would be released, she started to relax. "Bullshit, Sam, I could just see you putting up ten grand without us coming up with no money. Why hell, Sam, you wouldn't do that for your poor old mother, let alone two poor blacks who have to make their money out in the streets." She took his arm as they started walking towards the door that led from the courtroom. "Yes," she said, "I'm afraid that that's the biggest damn lie you've told all week, but I must admit, it was sweet of you to say it."

"When you say things like that, Connie, you hurt me right here," Sam said with mock dignity, placing his hand over his heart for effect. A black couple walking past stared at them, and the man glared angrily at Connie. She laughed loudly as she realized what the man was probably thinking.

They walked out of the building arm in arm, laughing and talking happily. Sam led her across the street to his office. People sitting around stared at them as they entered and went into one of the offices.

Sam pointed towards a chair and Connie sat down, crossing her long, well-shaped legs. The short dress she wore had not been bought for concealment. Sam was interrupted from straightening out the papers on his desk by Earl's arrival. The lawyer was with him.

"No wonder it took so damn long for me to get my bond," Earl said kiddingly. "My old lady and the bondsman are hanging out over here in this crummy office playing games, while my lawyer knocks hisself out trying to get me the highest bond in town."

All three men laughed, then Milton asked, "Is everything ready, Sam?" He didn't wait for an answer. "Jesus Christ! Did you hear that son-of-a-righteous bastard? Ten-thousand-dollar bond! Of all the crap." Earl's attorney was really angry about the bond. Earl listened as Mills continued. "Sam, we're going to have to get this case out of that bastard's courtroom, you know, because you can't tell what that old bastard might do."

"You think you can swing it?" Earl asked quickly. He didn't look forward to going in front of the old man, either, because he would be the one to serve time if something went wrong.

"You're damn right I can handle it. If I can't get it changed, we'll just stall the case until that old bastard dies of old age."

Everyone in the office laughed.

"Well, come on, Sam, let's get the papers signed. My client hasn't got all day," the attorney said.

"You really must pay him a lot of money, Earl," Connie said lightly. "Either that or you owe him a nice piece of cash. I know from experience that that's the only thing that will make him *worry* about a client."

The bondsman laughed loudly, and Earl winked at Connie. "You really know him, honey," he said and removed a large sum of money from his pocket. "But Sam here, he's just as bad." Earl peeled five hundred dollars from his bankroll, then turned to Sam. "Sam, are you hip to this guy here?" he said and pointed over his shoulder at his lawyer. "I mean *really* hip to him?" he said, laying the five hundred on top of Sam's desk.

"Of course," Sam said and grinned. "Milton takes me to the golf course for lessons every weekend." The bondsman reached over and counted the money. "Well now, all we need is your little signature on the dotted line," he said, pushing some papers across his desk.

Milton moved close at the sight of the money, and Earl removed more money from his pocket. "Here," Earl said and held the money out towards his lawyer. "It ain't but three hundred in that roll, but it should give you peace of mind until I get you some more downtown."

The attorney counted the money greedily. "Don't forget, Earl, that leaves a balance of fifteen hundred now," the attorney said as the couple stood up and made ready to leave.

Earl didn't bother to answer. He steered Connie through the door. They took a cab, and Earl remained silent until after the cab had dropped them off and they had entered his penthouse. He shut the door and leaned against it. "Where the hell did you get five hundred dollars at, Connie?"

"That's the money me and Vickie made last night, daddy. I still got over a hundred dollars left." Connie reached down in her bra and removed the rest of the money. She counted the money before handing it over to Earl.

He jammed the money into his pocket and walked back into the bedroom. "There's close to a hundred and fifty dollars there, Earl," she called out gaily. From past experience, he knew she wanted to be loved for such a good night's work. His mind was on something else though. He ignored her and stripped down to his shorts. He grabbed a towel from the dresser and snatched up his bathrobe. In minutes, Connie could hear the sound of the shower running.

"Oh well," she murmured. She picked up his discarded clothing and removed everything from the pockets, placing his belongings on top of the dresser. She hung his clothes up neatly and put shoe trees into the shoes he had taken off. She then placed them in a rack in the closet.

When he emerged from the shower, water dripped slightly from his shoulders as he glanced around. He had known everything would be put away neatly, and when Connie came over and took the towel from his hand, he had known she would do that, too. He turned slightly so that she could wipe the water from his back. She kissed him lightly, and he twisted around, laughing. "You're supposed to be drying my back, honey, not washing it." He slipped his arm around her waist.

Her eyes began to glisten. She had hope now that this would be one of those days when Earl didn't send her right back home. She wet her lips teasingly. "We goin' have a party, daddy?" she asked. Her voice became husky.

He didn't bother to answer; he just stretched out on the bed. Connie hit a button at the front of the bed and music flooded the room from all four walls. She moved gracefully with the sound, removing her clothes. Earl lay on the bed and smoked a reefer as he watched her take off each garment to the beat of the music. She approached the bed from the foot, and sensation exploded in his limbs as she worked her way up his body.

10

CHARLES WATCHED EARL pace up and down the living room.

"I don't know what you're so worried about," Charles said, opening the subject that both men had ignored. "You done hired the best goddamn lawyer money can buy, so if it's any win for you in the deal, he should be able to do it."

"I'll be the first one to admit it, Charles. These whiteys have got me scared," Earl said. "Ain't no reason for me to fool myself, baby boy, when these honkies get a nigger downtown in their courtroom, he ain't got no way of knowing how he goin' come out—lawyer or not."

Charles snorted. "Just relax, baby. You got it on your mind, that's your problem."

"It's not just that what's bothering me," Earl answered after a moment's thought. "It's Fay's funky ass that I'm thinking about. It's been two weeks now and they ain't released her yet."

"Shit," Charles answered sharply. "You ought to know damn well they're going to keep her locked up for a witness until they bring you to trial." Charles frowned, then added, "That's damn near standard procedure whenever there's a pandering case."

Earl slumped down on the couch. "You're sure of that shit, huh?" He waited for Charles to reply, then added, "They didn't do that to Baby Ray's woman. They let her out. And Baby Ray tightened the bitch up before they went back to court, so that they had to toss the case out the fuckin' window."

"That was at a different time. This is an election year, and they'll do everything they can," Charles said. "Besides, they got that damn *bitch* on the city council now, and she's some kind of nut when it comes to whores."

"That bitch is just nutty when it comes to street whores," Earl managed to say. "I ain't heard her doing nothing about the macks behind the whores, just the bitches in the streets, that's all."

Both men stared at each other in silence for a moment. "I believe it goes a little deeper than that. She might not raise too much fuss about them white whores working 'cause when she's downtown at night, she can't tell that them white bitches riding by in them cabs is whores on their way to another hotel. But she can tell them black bitches working on them street corners down-town is whores, 'cause the bitches will try and stop a car no matter who's lookin' if it ain't no policeman," Charles said.

"That ain't got a damn thing to do with me and Fay."

"Don't fool yourself, Earl. That's just what this shit is about. Them people ain't crazy; they know some nigger is behind all them bitches out there in the streets. Why, they'd keep that fool-ass bitch of yours locked up for five years if it would help them to get your kind of nigger off the street. That's why I don't look for them to release her. They know, if you get your hands on that bitch, by the time your court date comes up you'll have that bitch in Georgia or somewhere."

Earl nodded. "You're right about that. If the bitch should have a change of heart, their case is thrown out the door. If you couldn't make the bitch change her mind, you could always pay somebody to kill the funky bitch," he said. Earl knew the right people to pay for such a job. He had been thinking constantly on this subject and now he put his thoughts into words. "You know what they do with men witnesses, don't you?"

"Yeah," Charles answered without thinking. "They generally make trusties out of them, if they want to work. That way they don't have to stay locked up, and they have the run of the place."

Earl was thoughtful for a minute. "Most all of the trusties I've ever run into were either selling

food they'd stole from out of the kitchen or selling cigarettes." Earl popped his fingers, then
asked, "You think that's what they done with her,
Charles?" He answered his own question. "Locked
her up as a material witness, then made a trusty
out of her."

"That's probably it, Earl. They pay her so much
a day and put it in her account for her until she
gets out."

Earl's temper flared. "The bitch is going to
need more than money! This thing between me
and the bitch ain't goin' be finished after no trial.
I'm going to do something to this bitch if it ain't
nothing but bust her fuckin' legs."

Charles spoke gravely. "By the time you get this
mess straightened out, you ain't hardly goin' want
any trouble out of that bitch, Earl."

Earl laughed before replying, but his thoughts
were completely different from the words he
spoke. "You may be right about that, Charles, because I wish now that I'd never met the crazy
bitch."

The telephone interrupted them. Earl picked
up the receiver. "Hold on, baby, and talk slower.
That's better, Doris, now I can understand what
you're saying."

Her words came to him more clearly. "I'm in
jail, Earl; they popped me this morning."

Doris glanced at the nearest matron and then
lowered her voice. "Early this morning, Earl, two
white bastards came to the door. I started not to

let them in, but they were dressed like hillbillies and they acted like they had been there before."

"Goddamn!" Earl roared. "Didn't I tell you not to let anybody in unless they call first?"

"They asked for Fay, Earl, so I figured they had been there before. Anyway, they came in, and I sold them some whiskey. Next, they tried to get me to call in another girl, but I put an end to that. I figured I wouldn't need any help turning two damn tricks, so I set the price at fifty dollars apiece, if they wanted to see me." She laughed lightly. "That was the magic word, baby. Out popped their badges, and here I am, uptight."

Earl laughed gaily. "Wonderful," he said. "Maybe my luck is beginning to change for the better."

Doris removed the receiver from her ear and stared at it. "I don't know what you mean by that, Earl, 'cause I can't see anything amusing about my being in here."

"Hold the line a minute, Doris," he said. He walked into the bedroom and closed the door, then picked up the extension phone. "Listen, baby, just listen. You're going into court first thing in the morning, and you ain't got no problem, 'cause my lawyer will be there with you on the case. So you know it won't be nothing but a fine."

Doris agreed. "I know it ain't nothing big, honey," she said.

Earl lit a cigarette and said between puffs, "After you get your fine tomorrow, Doris, I'm going to wait until the next day before I pay it and get you released."

"What?" Doris asked sharply, causing the ma- tron to stare at her quickly.

"Just listen," Earl interrupted sharply. "I think Fay's locked up somewhere on that floor they put all you women at. So this is what I want you to do. Make contact with the crazy bitch and promise her two thousand dollars, Doris, if she drops the charges on my case. Tell her she ain't got nothing to worry about—ain't nobody going to harm her for the trouble she done caused me. Just tell her, baby, that if she don't drop the charges, she might as well make up her mind to stay where she's at until this time next year, 'cause my lawyer's goin' have the fuckin' case postponed until hell freezes over."

Before Doris could answer, the matron spoke up harshly. "I done told you once, girl, that your time is up. So how about us hanging up the phone like a nice girl?"

"Okay, okay, miss. Earl? I'll have to go now. The turnkey is raising hell about me staying on the phone too long, but I understand what you want, so don't worry. If I get the chance, I'll take care of everything. You know I still love. . . ." The phone went dead in Earl's ear. The matron had cut the line.

Doris' temper flared at the matron's action. She dropped the receiver down hard on the woman's hand. "Ouch!" the big, heavyset woman screamed. Anger leaped into her eyes, and for a brief moment she started to strike Doris. She managed to control her anger. "Okay, dearie," she said slowly, "looks like we're going to have a little problem with you, but I promise you, we can handle anything you put down." The matron had been working in the women's prison ward for five years, and she had dealt with some of the meanest women in the city. To her, Doris had the look about her of a dangerous woman. She stepped back and nodded. "That way, dearie."

Without hesitation, Doris started walking in the direction the matron's finger pointed. She halfheartedly listened to the woman's voice behind her as they walked.

"You know, dearie, you can make it easy or hard on yourself—that's up to you—but the next time you fuck up and slam a receiver down on my hand, we're going to find out just how tough you really are."

"Yeah, *dearie,*" Doris replied, using the term the matron used all the time. The woman guard, known by all the female prisoners as the beast, put her hands on her hips when Doris stopped in front of her cell.

"*Oh* no, dearie, not yet. First you take that mop, and then find you a bucket and see how well you can mop up this corridor."

"Shit," Doris snorted, then wrinkled up her nose and stared thoughtfully at the large, muscular matron. It was better to be doing something than to be locked up in her tiny cell, she reasoned. Before the matron changed her mind, she grabbed up the mop and found a bucket in an empty cell. She filled the bucket with water while in the cell, then carried it out into the corridor.

The matron watched her closely as she began to mop up the long corridor, then turned around and found her soft chair at the front of the ward. All she had to do was lean over the desk to see whatever Doris was doing. All of the cells containing prisoners were locked. The open cells were all empty. Either the women who lived in the open cells were preoccupied with simple jobs like the one Doris was doing or no one had moved in yet. Some of the women were out on hospital call or gone to see the prison dentist.

In the very last cell, Fay lay propped up on her elbow, glancing through an old magazine. "Well, I'll be damned. Look what the fuzz drug in out of the rain! Miss *fine* herself."

Doris stared into the cell. Her eyes became near slits. She managed to control her temper before she spoke. "Well, well, well. If it ain't our number-one informer for our not-too-famous police department. How does it feel to be locked up for nothing, honey? Huh?"

Fay shrugged her shoulders. Her hair was tangled and she seemed listless. "You were there, Doris. You saw what that nigger did. He didn't have to *kick* me. What did you think I was goin' do, accept it?"

Doris leaned her mop against the cell door.

"Listen, sweetie, maybe he was wrong in kicking you, but you're not hurt now. Do you think I would want to lay down here in this funky jail for damn near a year just to put a nigger man in jail? If he had kicked you down the stairs or something, Fay—maybe breaking your arm or something like that—I might could understand this shit, but just an ass kickin'? Any good whore can stand one every now and then. Besides, it might teach you something."

"Ain't that a bitch!" Fay said as she got up off the bunk. She walked to the front of the cell and gripped the bars tightly. "If you can't understand it, Doris, that's too damn bad. I don't care if I have to stay locked up for two years—let alone one— I'm going to put Earl's black ass right where he belongs."

Both women glared at each other. Doris tried to make her voice stay calm. "You're mistaken, Fay. A whore ain't never got to bust her man for pandering. That's just helping the white man out. Why, it's too easy for you to choose another man without getting mud all over your name the way you're getting it on yours, bitch." Both women fell silent for a minute, then Doris continued. "What you need, whore, is a man carrying a lunch pail filled with dry sandwiches to some little job every day, 'cause you ain't qualified, bitch, to have no motherfuckin' pimp. A nigger sportin' diamond rings, wearing silk suits, and driving a Caddie is way out of your league, you sorry-ass bitch!"

Fay turned her back on Doris and walked to the back of the cell. "You can say what you want to say, Doris, but it ain't goin' keep so-called Earl the Pearl's black ass out of the joint. You can bet on that."

Doris picked up her mop and said softly, "If you forget about those charges, Fay, as soon as you get out, all you got to do is stop at Earl's lawyer's office and he'll hand you two thousand dollars so that you can go anywhere your heart desires."

"Fuck that shit! I don't want to go nowhere but to court and see them bury Earl's funky ass behind some of these same kind of bars, and you can tell him for me, I'll wait with exquisite patience until that day."

The matron put down the book she had been reading and glanced over her desk just in time to see Doris dragging the mop in front of Fay's cell. "Goddamnit, girl, is that all you've mopped in all this time?" she asked loudly.

Doris glanced down the corridor at the matron, but didn't bother to answer. Her mind was too busy on other matters. She moved with the mop as if she were a robot, until her actions satisfied the guard. Fay's sarcastic laughter rang down the long hall, and after the sound had died, Doris could still hear it ringing shrilly in her ears.

The night passed slowly for Doris. She tossed and turned on her narrow cot all night. On two occasions, the night matron found her standing and holding onto the bars. She was sitting on her bunk smoking when daybreak began to peep through the prison cells from the tiny windows overhead. She was wide awake when they called her name to go over to the hospital for her medical examination. This was standard procedure for all prostitutes incarcerated. Whenever they were picked up, the city gave them a checkup in their battle to keep down V.D. If a girl was found to have a disease, the court would automatically give the woman six months. The girls were led handcuffed to the hospital, where they waited in line nervously for the doctor to give them their clearance.

"Judy Blender," a nurse called. A slim, dark-complexioned Negro girl stood up and waited for the matron to relieve her from the handcuffs. She then followed the nurse into the doctor's small treatment room. The remaining six girls glanced at each other nervously. They knew what it meant when the nurse called you into the treatment room. You had to go and get a shot, then the nurse marked your card in big red letters, showing the world that you had a dose, or something worse.

When Judy came out of the treatment room, it seemed as if Doris heard them calling her name from a far distance. It couldn't be, she thought wildly, but sure enough, it was. As she followed the nurse, she cursed herself inwardly. She knew what had happened, and when. She had thought the trick was having a premature discharge from too much handling. She had been sure of it because she had had to play with the john to make him want to spend any money. He had been waiting for his friend, but she had insisted that he do something after his friend finished. She remembered how red the trick had got in the face when the come had come out of the head of his dick, but she still hadn't paid any heed. Greediness. That had been her reward, but she had wanted so bad to surprise Earl with as much money as possible. Well, one thing, she thought, she hadn't given the dose to Earl. That much was sure. She hadn't slept with the man yet, and from the way it seemed, it would be quite a while before she got the chance to lay up with him in the future. Goddamnit, she cursed inwardly. She didn't fear the six months, but she had wanted some of that dick so bad, and now it would seem like years before she got a chance to lay up with that sweet brown meat.

After they left the hospital, the matron took them to have breakfast. The rest of the women sat as far away from the two diseased women as possible. They acted as if something could rub off on them. Even the matron acted differently towards them. When they finished eating, she led them straight to court. There was a large bullpen right off the courtroom, and the matron locked all of the inmates inside of this large, empty cell. Inside of the bullpen, out of the sight of people who happened to be passing by, there was a sewer in the floor in the far corner of the cell. This was for the girls' use, if they should happen to want to use the toilet before court began. From it arose a strong odor, so most of the girls tried to keep their distance from it.

Most of the girls talked with assurance of their coming court appearance. "Shit, I ain't even worried. I know my daddy's goin' get me out. If money can get you, I'll sure be out of here." The talk continued, but Doris refused to be drawn into it.

One girl ventured to say, "Doris, your old man sure is in bad luck this month, ain't he? Here you are about to begin a six-month bit, and his other girl dropping a pandering charge on him. Shit, he ain't long for the streets with that kind of luck."

"Don't none of you bitches worry about Earl, honey. You can bet he will take care of hisself," she replied.

"I know damn well that judge is going to give me six months," Judy stated to no one in particular. She tried to start up a conversation with Doris, but again Doris remained out of it. Her thoughts were on Earl and nothing else. It seemed as if a fog was surrounding her mind. She felt as if the world was against her. After finally finding a man she could really love, something like this had to happen. She wasn't thinking about her problem, not in the least. What worried her was the possibility of Earl getting sent away to prison. If that happened, she felt as if she would just die. It was too much for her to endure. She knew if that happened, she'd track Fay's ass down and strump the shit out of her.

Suddenly she heard her name being called. She glanced up at the matron in surprise. "Come on, dearie," the beast said, sneering. "The judge won't wait forever, not even for a clapped-up whore." Harsh laughter followed her statement. She took Doris by the arm and led the way. They walked out into a crowded courtroom. It was as if they had entered another world.

The judge was handling another case as they came out, and the matron sat Doris down in an open pew. It reminded her of the hard benches they used to kneel down on in the Catholic church she attended when she was a girl.

Her lawyer, Milton, weaved his way through the courtroom. He stopped beside Doris and smiled down at her. "I've talked to Earl, dear, and he wants you to plead guilty. Is that your plea?"

Doris seemed to brighten at the mention of Earl's name. "You know it's whatever Earl wants, darling. You know that." She smiled up at Milton, then added, "You know I always do what my daddy wants me to do."

Milton grinned kindly. He was not surprised at the simplicity of the young woman. It was a rare occasion when he came in contact with one that wasn't completely obedient to her man. Sometimes he wished that he could demand and get the same respect from his wife that the pimps demanded from their women. Before the judge called her up, she told Milton about the dirty smear test she had had that morning. "Nothing to worry about," he had replied.

When the judge called her name, she followed Milton up to the bench. After he explained to the judge that she was going straight to her personal doctor, he let her off with a four-hundred-dollar fine. After that, she was quickly returned to the bullpen.

"What's going on out there today," one of the girls asked seriously. "Ain't the judge passing out no fines?"

The group of women fell silent as they waited for Doris to answer. If there were no fines, only flat time, then all of them would be facing house time, and none of them wanted that. Each of them began to remember the last time they had been brought downtown.

A narrow-chested woman stated loudly, "If he's passing out time, I'm finished, 'cause I was busted last week and just got a fine."

Doris spoke up finaily. "He gave me a four-hundred-dollar fine, and it wouldn't have been that high if I hadn't had that dirty test this morning."

"That's right," one of the girls said, "you had to have a shot this morning. Girl, you're lucky as hell. They usually give you six months for having a dirty smear. Shit, you're sure enough lucky. Four hundred dollars ain't bad at all."

The tension was broken and the girls began to talk and joke loudly. "I'm goin' go home and take me a bath as soon as I get cut loose," one girl blurted out happily.

A young girl not over seventeen, with heavy makeup, spoke up loudly, "Hey, Doris, if that's the case, then what the hell are you doing back here? Don't tell me Earl the Pearl can't raise your fine money."

Some of the girls looked up in surprise. They hadn't thought about that. Four hundred was a large amount, but she didn't have a chili-bowl pimp; she had one of the big players. But facts were facts, and only the girls who couldn't pay their fines were returned to the bullpen.

Doris ignored the question and sat down. The young girl continued, "Honey, if you can't raise that much money, my old man might get you out. He wants a wife-in-law for me bad enough."

The other girls anticipated trouble, but Doris remained calm. "Honey, I appreciate your offer, but I don't need it. My man is well aware of what's happening, and so am I, so thanks anyway, okay?"

After that, the women left her alone. In about two hours there were only two women left in the bullpen: Doris and Judy. Judy received six months. "It's a goddamn shame," Judy said for the fifth time. "If that ignorant bastard I had for a man had got me a lawyer like yours did, I'd have gotten a fine instead of all this fuckin' time."

A young matron opened the door and led them

to the elevator, where two more matrons waited to take them across the street to their cells. When they got there, the heavyset matron who had put Doris to work the day before was on the desk. She took their files and read them quickly, then removed a ring of keys from a desk drawer. "You," she stated, pointing to Judy. "Don't walk too near me." She got up from behind the desk, wrinkling her nose. "You think I want some of that filth rubbing off on me?" she added harshly.

She took her keys and opened a cell door, pushing the door open wide and stepping back. "I guess you know I'll be glad to see your fast ass on the bus tomorrow heading for the state farm."

Judy swished into her cell. "I don't give a damn how happy you'll be. You can die in your goddamn sleep tonight for all I care!"

Doris laughed. The matron quickly turned on her. "You're just as filthy as she is. The very sight of either of you reminds me of something dirty."

Before Doris could reply, the matron spoke up sharply. "None of your smart mouth now! We didn't ask you to come down here." The older woman stared at Doris as if she had been personally offended. "And don't think because you didn't pay your fine you're going to have it made and just lay around either. Come along," she said, leading her towards the kitchen.

Fay lay on her bunk with her legs crossed high in the air. She tossed a book violently into the corner and then stood up and stretched. The black skirt she wore came up above the top of her rolled-up stockings. She stared into the mirror the police had provided her with and straightened out her blonde wig. Without really meaning to, she stared around the bleak cell. Her thoughts were cold and bitter. I'm going to have to get out of here, she thought for the thousandth time. After sleeping, she regretting having spoken so sharply to Doris. The two thousand dollars would have made up for a lot of things.

The sound of the coffee wagon arriving caused Fay to react automatically. She turned, picked up her drinking cup, and stepped to the front of the cell. The fleeting thought of contacting the detectives and changing her story flashed vividly across her mind. If she did that, she reasoned, they just might release her later that evening. Out of the corner of her eye, she saw Doris step towards her, carrying a pitcher of steaming coffee. She smiled at the approaching woman. I'd better tell her I've changed my mind, she thought.

Without missing a step, Doris tossed the hot pitcher. The scalding coffee streamed towards Fay, enveloping her. A scream started in Fay's throat and got stuck there, but as the scalding liquid splashed against her, a scream burst from deep inside her, and she continued to scream as the hot liquid splashed into her face and saturated her clothing, blistering her from head to foot.

11

EARL DROVE EXPERTLY through the traffic until he reached Twelfth Street. The top was down on his convertible and he waved gaily at two women working out of a gangway.

One of the women yelled out to him, "Why don't you park and do some business, honey?" Earl laughed as he parked the car, and the women joined in the laughter with him. He got out and walked in to the Gilbert Hotel, a combination bar and hotel. He took a mental note of Billy's and Carl's Cadillacs sitting at the curb. He stopped at the desk, where an elderly Negro woman sat. "I think Vickie is inside the bar," she informed him.

"Thank you, Mrs. Jones," Earl replied to the woman. He opened a door off the lobby and entered the lounge, stopping inside the door to allow his eyes to get accustomed to the darkened room. There was a horseshoe-shaped bar inside the club. The barmaids worked with a small stage separating them. Billy and Carl were sitting with Vickie between them. Earl stopped right behind them.

Vickie seemed to feel his presence, because she turned and smiled. He was again taken aback by the beauty of her smile. It was like the coming of dawn in a starless night. It was uncanny, and it was inconceivable to him that he had allowed himself to fall in love. He couldn't believe it.

"Don't you think you're keeping bad company, honey?" he said lightly in her ear. As he took her arm and raised her from the stool, he added, "These fellows ain't spendin' a penny, baby."

As she stood up, she lowered her eyes. The dazzling smile disappeared. "I was just sitting down here having a drink by myself, daddy, when they came in and sat down beside me."

Billy spoke up. "Don't worry about a thing, Vickie. If that's all he wants, I'll spend some money with you," he said seriously.

"Bullshit!" Earl said. "His money don't go, baby." He pulled her to him tightly and kissed her on the neck. "From now on, honey, when these snakes come down on you like that, you just go back upstairs and wait for me there, 'cause they ain't nothing but dogs, okay?" He didn't wait for an answer; he patted her on the rear and started her towards the stairway.

Billy watched the attractive young girl walk off

with her firm step. "That's right, Earl, you watch that one, 'cause I'd sure spend some money with her and try and steal her from you."

"Don't you think you treated us kind of cold in front of her?" Carl said. "You damn near gave the impression that you don't trust your ladies around your real friends!"

Earl grinned, amused. He pushed the Coke Vickie had been drinking towards the barmaid, who stood holding a bottle of champagne. He nodded, giving her the go-ahead with her selection, and she set the bottle down on the bar and opened it quietly. Earl glanced from Carl to Billy, who was still watching Vickie as she disappeared through the swinging doors. "Should I trust you guys?" he asked. All three men burst out laughing at the same time.

"We ain't got no conspiracy going to steal your girl, Earl," Billy managed to say between bursts of laughter. "But I would spend some money with her, and that's the God's truth."

"I know you would," Earl replied honestly, "but to be honest with you, Billy, I just don't want teeth marks all over that fine stuff." Earl's remark caused Carl to fall all over the bar laughing. The barmaid, overhearing their remarks, blushed, and Billy and Earl fell into each other's arms laughing at her embarrassment.

Billy replied, leering at the barmaid, "You shouldn't mind me gettin' a little gash in my moustache." he said loudly.

Carl, turning up a glass of whiskey at the time, choked on his drink and spit whiskey all over the bar. The barmaid glanced around desperately. The other barmaid glanced over at her and shrugged her shoulders. This was something that happened every day as far as she was concerned; she only wished they had sat on her end of the bar because they always tipped good.

As the drinks flowed, the slight anger Earl had felt when he entered the bar disappeared. The ribbing continued. Carl turned on the attractive barmaid. "Girl, why don't you hang that apron up and get you some big money?"

The barmaid was a slim, brown-skinned girl in her late twenties. "If you're talking about getting money the way I *think* you're talkin' about, I don't need it that bad," she answered, putting her hands on her hips.

"You must need it pretty bad; you're here pouring drinks every day," Carl stated coldly.

The girl's eyes blazed. "My husband rather likes for me to make it this way, do you mind?" she asked sharply.

Carl raised up on his elbows and stared over the bar at her legs. "Girl," he said rolling his eyes, "with all that going for you, I must say your husband is making a mistake."

With a shrug of her shoulders, the barmaid walked off. She knew she didn't have a chance trying to compete with the men verbally. She stopped and spoke to Carl over her shoulder. "Here comes my husband in the door now, so you can be the first to tell him he ought to make a whore out of me."

Carl jumped and stared at the empty doorway. Earl burst out laughing. "You damn near jumped off that bar stool, man. Your nerves must be damn near shot."

Billy poked Earl in the ribs. "That's the last thing Carl would want to see is an angry husband."

"I'll second that statement," Carl answered quickly. He was a man who loved humor, even when he was on the receiving end. His broad face spread wide with a grin. "You guys know me. I'm a lover, not a heavyweight." The barmaid came back and removed Earl's empty champagne bottle from its bucket. There was a small amount left, so she poured it for herself.

"That's one of the reasons why I'd never pimp for my man," she stated dryly. She raised the glass and drank the wine down.

"That's a word you shouldn't use so lightly, lady," Earl said as he watched her closely. "So many of you working ladies use that word so loosely—'man' —without really knowing what a real man is."

The barmaid laughed harshly. "My idea of a good man, honey, is one who can hold down two jobs without missing a day."

"I figured that," Earl replied coolly. "But what you really mean is you need a mule for a husband, not a man." Earl reached across the bar and grabbed her arm before she could walk away. "Wait a second, honey. If a nigger lays his game on you right, you won't be worried about how many jobs he can hold down. In fact, you probably wouldn't let him go out the door and work."

Her faced worked up in a frown, and she stared at Earl as if he had just climbed from under a rock. She managed to pry his fingers from her arm. "That nigger ain't been born yet!" she said as she walked off.

"Fuck that bitch!" Billy said loudly. "She must think her cock is made out of gold."

Carl became serious. "I hear you been having your problems, Earl. I was wondering how Doris came out of that shit downtown, man."

"Yeah, man," Billy said. "I heard about that treacherous bitch, Doris, trying to scald Fay. Did she do a good job of it?"

Earl replied slowly. "Yeah, she burned the bitch up pretty bad. It must have been, 'cause I had to put up a ten-thousand-dollar bond to get the bitch out."

"What did she burn the bitch with?" Billy asked curiously. "I heard she got scalded, but with what?"

"Coffee," Earl said. "The crazy bitch tossed a pitcher of hot coffee in on top of Fay. I ain't seen Fay yet, but I hear she's burned bad—in the face."

"These crazy things the bitch is doing, it ain't from your personal guidance, is it?" Carl asked.

"I'm sure ya'll don't think I'm behind this shit, do you? If I was, I wouldn't have told the bitch to burn her, I'd have instructed her to kill the funky bitch. That way I wouldn't have no more trouble out of her."

Billy quickly agreed with him. "That's what you needed, Earl, for that fool-ass bitch to go and die on you." He thought for a moment, then added, "If it's one thing I hate, it's one of those police-calling bitches! The whore needs to be killed, that's what the whore needs."

"That bitch needs killing a thousand times, if you ask me," Carl said. "When that little commotion started at my place, Earl, if I'd had the slightest idea that bitch was goin' start big trouble like this, I'd went on and had something did to her funky ass. If you get any more problems like this, Earl, even a big bankroll will start to feel the pressure."

"*Begin* to feel it?" Earl said sharply. "Listen, man, between my lawyer and bondsman, there went my bankroll. And that ain't no bullshit." He turned to Billy. "Did you bring my package, brother?" Without waiting for an answer, Earl removed his bankroll and peeled off one thousand dollars. He placed the money on Billy's leg.

Without hesitation, Carl followed suit. He handed a roll of money to Billy, as Billy checked the mirror to see if anyone in the large barroom had witnessed the transaction. There was no indication that anyone had taken the slightest interest in what was happening between the men at the bar; not even the barmaids had noticed anything. Billy caught the eye of a tiny brown-skinned woman sitting in a booth at the rear of the club. She came out of the booth slowly. Earl had never even noticed the woman in the club. He had thought the booth was empty.

"How is Doris doing, Earl?" the woman asked as she joined the men at the bar. She stood between Billy's legs and smiled at the men.

"Oh, how you been doing, Sandra? I didn't even recognize you, girl. Doris is getting along just fine," Earl said, answering her question. He saw her slip something into Billy's pocket, then continued. "I got her out on bond yesterday, you know."

"Well, now, that is good news. Tell her I said to look for me. I'm going to stop by and see her one day this week." Sandra waved at Carl. "Hi there, big fellow. You're not going to sit there and not even speak to me, are you, Carl?" Before he could answer, she reached up and pulled Billy's head down so that she could whisper something in his ear. "Bye now," she said to the men as she made her way from the bar. Her jacket pocket bulged as if she had a large roll of money stuck in it.

Billy removed two small packages from his pocket. He slid one to Earl, then pushed the other one to Carl. "Well now," he said quietly, "I might as well let you guys carry your own weight. The football now belongs to you, and so does the worry." He tossed a fifty-dollar bill on top of the bar. "I guess I can afford to take care of the bar tab this time, brothers. Barmaid?" he yelled. "Get off your ass, girl, and earn your money. Take a five-dollar bill for yourself, honey, and use the rest of the money to keep the bar full of drinks."

Carl grabbed his arm before he walked away. "How many cuts can I put on this shit, man?" he asked nervously.

"It's just like I told you, baby, you can cut the stuff four times and still have a beautiful blow. Just don't use too much damn quinine on the shit," Billy said as he got up from the bar. "You sure don't know when whore money runs short and the pimps have to go into other businesses to keep their heads above the water," he said before leaving the bar.

The other two men watched him walk away. Carl stood up and straightened his tie. "Don't look like he wasted much time getting away, does it?" he asked no one in particular.

"Fuck it," Earl said and felt the small package of dope resting in the palm of his hand. The dope made him restless too. He knew why Billy had gotten away so quickly. Whenever you had dope on you, it was time to make a move. You didn't loiter with it, unless you were a damn fool.

"Every time I have to handle some of this shit," Carl said suddenly, "I get nervous as hell. My mind plays some of the damnedest tricks on me. I start to believing the police are behind every door or waiting around the corner for me."

Both men joked for a minute, but neither wasted any time. When Carl felt that Billy had had enough time to be away from the place, he made his move. Billy was the only one of them known by the police as a drug man. The others were believed to be nothing but pimps. "Later baby," he said and departed.

"Take care of yourself," Earl yelled. He hadn't had to wait, since he had an apartment on the second floor, but he knew that Carl was trembling, so he had stayed to keep the big man company. Vickie opened the door instantly when he knocked. The hotel apartment had a Murphy bed, one that came out of the wall. Vickie had the bed down, but she had taken the time to make it up neatly, so Earl had an idea of what she had in mind. He sat on the end of the bed and began to mix up his drugs. He kept his milk sugar and other things he used to fix up his drugs in Vickie's apartment since she didn't generally turn any tricks out of there.

She watched him mix up the drugs with fear in her heart. She was not naive or inexperienced enough not to be aware of what he was doing or how much time he could get if he got busted for handling drugs. They would throw the book at him because they wanted him already.

"Oh baby, daddy, do you have to do this?" she pleaded. "I mean, can't we work something else out?" She walked over to the bed and climbed up behind him and placed her hands on his shoulder, but he quickly shook them off. For some reason, she couldn't keep her hands off him. Whenever he came around, she had an overwhelming desire to always put her hands somewhere on him. She had never felt this way about anyone in her brief life.

"If you need something to do, woman, try folding up each one of these packages as I finish with them."

After about twenty minutes, they finished the packaging of the drugs. It had been a slow job and a dull one. Earl took his time and counted out each one of the packages of narcotics. "Damn it," he said without anger. "I couldn't get but fifty-five quarters out of my investment. If everything goes right, I should make somewhere in the neighborhood of twenty-five hundred dollars. That ain't too bad," he continued, as if he were talking to himself. "If I get rid of it quick, it won't be no problem." He removed a ten-dollar bill from his pocket. "Take this downstairs, Vickie, and rent another room in this joint for the night."

Vickie took the money and hurried off on her errand. Earl waited impatiently for her return. He knew she would move as fast as possible, but it still seemed as if it took her hours when, in fact, she was gone only ten minutes.

She returned panting, as if she had run, which she had. She came to the door of the apartment and beckoned for Earl, and he followed her out into the hallway. He didn't give a damn what the place looked like that she had rented, but it seemed to make her happy, so he followed. She opened the door slowly. Earl walked into the room and examined the place carefully. It would do—here or elsewhere—it didn't make any difference.

"Vickie, I want you to stay in this room tonight. I'll be calling back to check on you." He raised his hand for silence. "Now dig, baby, what I want you to do is this. Each time I call back, I'll be sending someone over to pick up one of these packages of dope, so you'll know in advance who's coming and who to let in."

"Don't worry about me, daddy, I know how to handle myself in the streets."

"Well, this ain't the streets, girl, so just listen. Each time I call, you're to go down the hall and pick up one package. I'll let you know over the phone if you'll need more than one at a time. Now, each time a customer comes, he or she will be spending fifty-five dollars or more. I'll be out in the streets drumming up business, and if everything goes right, by daybreak we'll have a pocketful of money."

He reached out and pulled her to him, holding her tightly in his arms. "I don't like this, baby, but it has to be done." He released her but still held her hand, leading her out into the hallway and back to their other apartment. Once they got inside, he picked up the dope and searched for a hiding place. His fingers dug down into the dirt of a large flower pot. He scraped enough dirt out so that his package could fit down inside the hole he had dug. Then he covered the drugs up carefully and replaced the flower pot on the window sill.

"What about those?" Vickie asked, pointing at packs lying on the floor. Without answering, Earl picked up the drugs and tied them tightly in his handkerchief.

Earl tossed the small bundle up in the air and caught it neatly as it came down. "These are the ones you are going to start out selling, Vickie, baby." He reached out again and pulled the sepia-complexioned woman into his arms. Damn, he thought as he held her tight, I can't keep my hands off of her. He kissed her gently. "Now don't you worry about nothing, honey," he said as he pushed her out to arm's length.

"I'm not worried about myself, daddy. I just don't want nothing to happen to you out there in the streets." It never entered her mind that, with her selling the drugs, the chances of something happening to him were very remote, while her danger of being arrested or robbed was great.

She stood back on her heels and stared up into his dark eyes. "What you thinking about, daddy? You sure look serious enough."

He returned her stare without blinking and lied. "I was wondering if I should keep you out of this shit, Vickie, and handle it all myself." Before she could interrupt, he added, "I could do it without too much trouble, you know."

Her reactions were just what he expected, but it still hurt him a little to realize that he had all this tender love and had to exploit it.

"Don't draw the line on me now, daddy, please," she pleaded, and there was a note of desperation in it.

"Okay, baby, okay. But remember one thing, don't let nobody in that I haven't told you was coming over. Nobody. Do you understand that?"

She nodded in agreement and laid her head on his chest. He lifted her head and planted a kiss gently on her lips. Her tongue flicked out and he could feel burning fire inside his mouth. The passion in her kiss warmed his very soul. He moaned as she pressed against him tightly. He could feel her heavy thighs pressing against him. She moved her hips and he could feel the heat from her body. The tight mini-skirt slipped down and she stepped out of it. He didn't realize how she had gotten out of it. He didn't realize that it was his own fingers that slowly unsnapped her bra. Her firm, young breasts sprang out, and he lowered his head and took one of the golden brown gifts into his mouth and rolled it on the tip of his tongue. He played with the nipple until it became hard, then he ran his hands up between her legs and rubbed slowly until she moaned with inconceivable anguish. An unwholesome heat ran down his spine as she stuck her tongue in his ear. He fell back on the bed with her clasped tightly in his arms. Saliva ran from his mouth as he tried to pull her young head up from his stomach. He didn't want it that way. He wanted to penetrate her, he wanted to pound furiously into her belly. He rolled her over and straddled her wildly. His penis became enormous. He forced it between her legs. She screamed out in pain. This wasn't the kind of love he was used to. He wasn't using any of his vast experience. It was animal lust. He took her the way a stallion took a mare. He didn't give nature time to moisten her before he forced his way in. She screamed again, but his passion was so intense that it didn't make any difference. Her animal instincts came alive then, and she met him thrust for thrust, pain for pain, and soon it was scream for scream as she dug her nails in deeply and drew blood from his quivering back.

It didn't last long, and soon they both lay on their backs staring up at the ceiling. "Damn," he managed to say, "I ain't never carried on like that before, Vickie. I don't know, woman, you must have your mojo workin', girl."

She smiled, savoring the encounter. "It really was something else, honey. We ain't never did nothing like that before, and I ain't in no hurry to ever do it again."

"I'll go along with that!" he agreed quickly. He

twisted her around in his arms and started to take her slowly and gently. They made love this time with care. She groaned and moaned softly. Her voice was a caressing murmur in his ear. When they reached their climax, they both came to-gether. There was no violence, only love. He held her tightly in his arms, feeling something he had never really felt before with a woman. "Vickie . . . ," he started to say that he loved her, but he couldn't get the words out.

"Yes, baby," she answered quietly. "What you want, honey?"

He took her arms from his neck, and slowly got out of the bed. He walked over to the mirror and glanced at his back. "Damn!" he swore as he stared at the scratch marks. "I ain't never been scratched up like that." He shook his head in wonder. This was something he never allowed any of his women to do. Once one of them started to scratch, he stopped making love to them. If she continued to scratch, she'd have to find her an-other love partner, because he just wouldn't stand for it. He hated to be scratched up, and didn't bite his tongue about it either. Either a woman did like he said or she didn't have him. That was that. Earl took a quick shower. When he came out, Vickie was sitting up in bed reading.

"Listen, Vickie. I want you to pay attention now. Whoever comes up here will be spending at least fifty-five dollars apiece for just one of these packs. Be sure don't nobody see where you keep your bags hid." He slipped his coat on and walked to the door. "Get ready to be a very busy woman for the next twenty-four hours," he said, closing the door behind him.

12

DARKNESS WAS INVADING the evening, shrouding figures in shadows, and the streets were becoming less crowded as the elderly hurried to the shelter of their small rooms or, if more fortunate, their small homes. Areas where children had played happily now became darkly ominous spots that women walked around with hurried steps.

Earl stopped his car in front of a large, run-down apartment building. He spoke politely to two elderly women sitting in folding chairs enjoying the evening air. The building he entered didn't have an elevator, so he walked the four flights up. He knocked lightly on the door of an apartment.

"Who the hell is it?" called a belligerent voice from inside. Earl quickly replied.

"Earl who?" asked the voice, now closer to the door.

An eye peeped out at Earl from a hole in the door. "Who you want to see, man?" a new voice asked.

"I want to see Super Sport," Earl replied, not liking the changes he had to go through.

There were shuffling noises behind the door before it finally opened. An old schoolmate stood in the door with a wide grin on his face. He pushed his hand out towards Earl. "Come on in, man, come on in. What is this?" he asked, smiling. "At first, I couldn't believe it was really you, Earl. Not the big fellow down here in the ghetto, man."

Earl stepped into the shooting gallery and stared up at Super Sport as the big man closed the door and put the bolts in place. The big man hadn't changed much over the years, Earl thought, except that the football build, which had made him the idol of the girls in school, was now turning to fat.

For a brief moment, Earl let his eyes drift around the apartment. It was something out of a horror show to the unaware. Junkies sat around the room with needles hanging from their arms. One young girl was bleeding from too many needle jabs that didn't hit paydirt. She continued to try desperately to hit a main. A young boy sitting beside her and nodding lifted a piece of cotton from the floor that someone had been using to wipe blood with. He moved the soiled cotton across her arm and tried to stop the blood from dropping onto her clothes.

She snarled at him like a cat. "Goddamn you,

Judd! I had a hit, motherfucker, and you done went and blowed it."

The boy stopped trying to wipe the blood away. "I didn't mean to hit your spike, bitch, but I care less than a fuck if you bleed to death. Just don't get no blood on the skirt—you ain't finished paying for it yet," he warned her, then dropped his chin back to his chest.

There was a smell in the room that, for a minute, Earl couldn't make out. Then it came to him that it was the smell of blood. There was an unwholesomeness about the apartment, and he wished his business was completed. His imagination had not prepared him for this.

"Well, Earl," Super Sport said quietly, "since you done had a good look around, and now you know how the other brothers and sisters live, tell me what brings you around my way. I know you ain't started using, have you?"

Perspiration broke out on Earl's forehead, and for a minute he couldn't understand what Super Sport was saying. He caught a grip on himself and said, "No, man, it ain't nothing like that. What I came by for was to let you be the first to know that I had some bomb stuff, man. Some sure-nuff good jive."

Super Sport laughed loudly. "You pimps kill me. You try and make everybody believe the whores would die if you didn't exist to accept their money, and then every damn one of you end up juggling with some dope bag. Yet every time I see one of you in a bar or somewhere, you guys are always talkin' that crap about the only kind of money you'll accept is whore money." Super Sport raised his voice at the end, and a few of the addicts sitting around overheard what he said and laughed.

Earl made a move towards the door.

"Wait a minute!" Super Sport said. "Where you going in such a rush, man?"

Earl stopped at the doorway and spoke so quietly that no one could overhear what he said. "I told you, man, I had some smack. Now, if you want to get your kicks panning me, I'll come back after I take care of this business and let you go for your busters."

Super Sport snorted. "If you goin' be a dope man, baby, be one. You got to tuck your sensitive feelings away, man, 'cause all you goin' be dealing with is dogs."

"Okay, man, I dig it," Earl replied. He wrote a number down. "Here, man, when you get ready to make up again how about trying out my stuff?"

"Hold your horses, baby," Super Sport said and grinned. "Man, ain't you hip? I'm always ready to get when some good smack is on the set, man. If you'll wait until I get through shootin' this cooker full of stuff, man, I'll spend eight hundred dollars with you. It ain't all the money in the world, but I spend that much twice a day, baby." Super Sport sat down and pulled up his sleeve, revealing needle tracks all over his arm from the use of drugs.

"I ain't got to lay, Supe. All you got to do is call that number, man, I got somebody there to take care of whatever you want."

Super Sport stared at Earl. "I know you have, man. I'll bet my last dollar you got one of your frail whores sitting in a room somewhere on top of all that dope." His harsh laughter followed Earl into the hallway. "What you better get hip to, Earl, is that this is the dope game and not the pimp game, baby. You better put some protection on that girl you got selling that stuff before somebody goes through there and takes her head off. But no matter, man, whatever happens. I'm going to give you a play." He grinned at Earl, then added, "Why, who knows? I might even end up buying me some trim instead of some stuff."

Earl was angry. He knew that Super Sport was just high, but it didn't help his conscience any by telling himself that. He stumbled going down the stairway and ended up leaving the building in a blind rage. For a second, he just sat in the car and stared straight ahead. He wished now that he had never bought the damn drugs, but he didn't really know that much about them. He started the motor up and rode around smoking some reefer until his mood changed. After that, he moved in and out of dopehouses for the rest of the night.

Sometimes he would call Vickie twice in less than ten minutes about some business coming through. At one time in the night, he had stopped and picked up drugs and carried them himself, selling them as he went along until the morning dawn caught him just about out of stuff and with a pocketful of money. When he staggered out of the last dopehouse on his schedule, he let out a sigh of relief. He felt humble after all the anguish and misery he had witnessed. He took his time and locked his car up slowly and carefully. As he went around the car, a police car drove slowly by, and the two officers stared at him suspiciously.

Earl laughed after they had passed. "I beat you that time," he yelled loudly. "I stuck my head in the devil's mouth that time and got away with it." He laughed to himself and staggered up to his apartment.

Vickie met him at the door. "You look mighty sexy for a gal who has been up for the past two days, honey," he said as he took her in his arms and kissed her.

She pretended to frown, but a smile burst from her as she nodded towards the pile of money on the table. "I think I'd rather sell the white poison, Earl, than go back to whoring." She added hurriedly, "I ain't never made so much money in so quick a time. I mean, you know, Earl, big money, like we got off that stuff."

He stared at her silently before replying. "I hadn't planned to handle any more than those first pieces of stuff, Vickie. But I listened to you and flipped my money again, and now we got twice as much as I needed, baby. We don't need no more parts of any dope, honey. We done got over the hump."

He motioned towards the money on the dresser. "No, baby, we don't need to handle no more drugs."

Vickie smiled happily as she opened the closet door. She rummaged around until she found what she was looking for. She wiggled out of her clothes and slipped the see-through gown over her head. "How do you like me in this?" she asked as she turned towards him.

Earl twisted around in his chair and had to catch his breath. The sheer black gown she wore seemed to be part of her body. With the wisdom of a woman, she had put on a red light, so the room held just the right shade of light for that moment. She drifted across the room towards him, and Earl held his arms out to her. The thought crossed his mind that he was supposed to have called Connie up, but he knew it was too late for that now. At that moment, Vickie seemed like the very creation of beauty, and she brought to his bedside a love that surpassed anything he had ever known before. Though they had been tired, they put records on and danced tightly in each other's arms, neither wanting to rush the morning that promised so much delight. As the music came to an end, they moved towards the bed together.

Vickie put both her arms around his neck and pulled his head down towards her heaving breasts. Her breathing became heavy, and her breath became a scorching heat wave in his ear.

"You know, daddy," she said huskily, passionately, "I'll do whatever you want. And any way you want me to do it."

"If that's the case, baby, how about turning loose that damn hammerlock you got on my neck?" he replied quickly. "I wouldn't want to do nothing or end up doing something that I didn't have any plans on doing," he said as she released him. He planted a kiss on her stomach, and she caught her breath and tightened up her muscles.

"Now is the time I should really give you a push," she said emotionally. Their laughter rang out, and he climbed into her waiting arms and pulled her tightly into his embrace.

13

RAIN SPATTERED DOWN against the window, and Earl rolled over and stared out in disgust. He climbed from bed slowly, walked to the window, and stared out at the darkened sky.

"It's one hell of a morning for a person to have to go to court, isn't it?" Doris asked. Her words had the same effect as thunder rumbling from the clouds.

Earl shook his head, trying to clear his thoughts. The heavy-hanging silence had stifled the air, heightened the glare of the ceiling lights, and moved the walls inward, sealing them in. He tried to shake off the mood. "It has been one hell of a weekend," he said, more to himself than to Doris. They had started out Friday evening giving a surprise party for her, and now he felt the after-effects of too much partying. But it was more than that, and he knew it. It was a warning. He felt that everything wasn't going to go like he hoped. The splashing rain on the window went unseen as flashes of the weekend came back to him. Charles and Vickie had danced so much that Charles' new woman, Tammy, had gotten mad and left. Earl remembered, smiling, the way Vickie moved when she danced. It was enough to make any woman jealous.

He frowned as he remembered that Billy and Pat had moved over to his couch and had started snorting dope. He'd have to have one of his girls clean it real good in case some of that shit had spilled on his cushions. He remembered suddenly that Connie had got a noseful of the dope, too. Thinking that it was coke, she had taken a big snort of the stuff. Then later in the evening, Connie and Vickie had tried to burn each other out on the dance floor. Earl pictured them vividly in his mind, bumping and grinding to the music, their short skirts pulled up high.

Carl had concentrated so hard watching the women dance, he had poured his drink in the lap of his date—another woman stormed from the penthouse angrily. After that, everyone had stayed on and partied until daybreak. Billy, so high he couldn't stand, kept yelling *"Showtime, show-time,"* after everyone had gone, until the girls got together and tossed him out the door. He had stood out in the hall and cursed, drunkenly, until the elevator stopped, then he staggered into it.

Earl hoped that he had made it home safely. He smiled to himself as he remembered the private show his girls had put on for him. Billy had been right, it was showtime.

He walked back to the bed, put his hand under the sheets, and rubbed Doris' leg as he remembered the part she had played in his private show. "That was some dance you put on, baby," he said, remembering the slow, tantalizing strip that had left nothing to the imagination. He had taken her to bed with him that morning, and her eyes had glistened like diamonds when he picked her over the rest of his girls.

Doris, grabbed his arm under the sheet and held it in one spot. Her eyes were smoking as she stared up at him. "Damn, daddy," she said in her deep voice, "all you have to do is touch me and I get hot all over."

Earl leaned over and kissed her playfully on the neck. His tongue flicked out expertly as he worked his way around her neck. The sound of Vickie and Connie stirring in the next room, thunder clapping and lightning flashing dangerously close, these things went unnoticed to the couple as their passion rose above the thunder.

Later, Earl lay back and waited for Doris to finish with her bath. He had taken his shower, leaving a little sooner than he usually did because of Doris. She was more mischievous this morning than she normally was. Earl wondered idly if she knew how hopeless it was for her to think she was going to get probation in court that morning. He clamped his teeth down on the end of his cigarette. "That goddamn lawyer," he cursed, helplessly. He thought about the deal he had been helplessly backed into. His lawyer had reached Fay, and she had promised to drop his case for a price. He had hoped that in time he would have been able to pay Fay to drop the charges against Doris, too, but the bitch wouldn't budge. The whore was pressing the case to the hilt.

A quavering feeling hit the pit of his stomach and left a bitter taste in his mouth. He couldn't get rid of the feeling that he was tossing Doris to the dogs in order to save himself. He shook his head like a dog shaking off water. He had tried, he thought, God how he had tried. He had spent big money trying to buy it, with no real results coming from his efforts, so now he had to accept the facts of life.

Playfully, Doris danced from the bathroom, her robe opening and closing, tantalizingly, as she stopped beside the bed. She appeared gay and carefree at the moment. Earl stood up and stared into her eyes. It was then that he could read the fear hidden behind the false air of gaiety.

A large lump formed in his throat preventing him from speech. He opened his arms and she fell into them. He held her tightly as she sobbed. "Don't worry, baby, ain't nothing as bad as it seems," he said, rubbing the back of her head softly. "Come on now, baby, give me a big smile. I think I smell bacon and eggs frying, so let's go and get our share."

It seemed to Doris as though her legs wouldn't carry her. I mustn't let Earl see me like this, she thought. Please, Jesus, please, she thought, let me be strong. Give me the strength to leave him without crying. She prayed as she followed him out of the bedroom.

Connie and Vickie had prepared enough food for the four of them, and the meal went quickly. Vickie tried to carry on a light conversation but soon gave up.

The phone rang. Connie called Earl to the phone. "It's Milton," she said and smiled at Doris. "Don't worry, honey, he's got the best lawyer in town on your case. Just leave it in their hands, okay?" The women smiled at each other, but there was a feeling of tension in the room.

Earl carried the phone into the bedroom. "Wait a minute," he said and closed the door so that no one could hear. "What you mean, man? All the money I've spent, and you mean to tell me that *now*, at this late date, you goin' pull my coat that you can't even get the *charge* lowered? That's got to be the stinkiest shit in town!"

"Just listen, Earl," the lawyer pleaded. "The judge this case came up in front of just won't listen, man! This case made headlines in the daily papers. It's a lot of people watching the results. A girl gets disfigured while in jail, then she drops the charges against you. Man, people are talking, and not just about this case. There are a few people who would like to hang your ass up to dry if they could."

"That's cold shit," Earl replied. "I ain't never known a peckerwood who wouldn't take money, man. I need my girl. She ain't no good to me off the streets, man. What good is a bitch to me doing time? Answer me that?"

"I'm sorry, Earl. I can't promise you anything on this one. Your girl will just have to take her chances," Milton said, then added, "Don't forget now, she has to be in court by ten. I'll be there waiting for you." Before Earl could say anything else, the lawyer hung up.

Both of the other women were already dressed. When Earl came out of the bedroom, Doris entered to get ready. Earl remained in his robe, since he had already explained to Doris why he couldn't be present. That was for the young pimps who weren't known—and who wanted to be known—to stand around in the back of the courtroom making everybody aware of them.

He walked over to the bar and poured a stiff drink, something he rarely did early in the morning. He drank the whiskey down without even tasting it.

The parting was as bitter as he had hoped it wouldn't be. Doris had clung to him tightly, not crying with sounds, just a flood of tears running down her cheeks. Connie and Vickie had managed to pry her arms from his neck, because he sure as hell couldn't get them loose. He hadn't really known what to do with her clinging so tightly to him. His eyes had darted around in desperation until Connie stepped forward and spoke calmly to Doris.

"Come on, honey, let's get on downtown so you can beat this thing and have it over with. Then we can come on home and pop some more."

After that, Doris had managed to gain some control. She walked towards the door, stopped and waved shyly to Earl. "In a minute, daddy," she had said.

This small touch on her part hit Earl like a sledgehammer. He staggered back to the bar as the women left and hung his head. His fingernails dug deeply into the wood until one of them broke, but he didn't notice it. He knew in his heart that she wouldn't be back, and he blamed himself for not being honest with her and telling her the truth.

Vickie was quiet as they came out of the court-room. Doris had been given five to fifteen years in prison. On the way out, Fay had stopped Connie and said something, making her mad. Vickie wondered idly about what had passed between the two women. Oh well, Connie would tell her in her own good time, she thought.

Connie waved a cab down, but it stopped across the street at the city hospital and picked up a passenger. Connie cursed as a car stopped in front of them, but Vickie smiled quickly at the white man behind the wheel. "Was you goin' give us a lift, darling?" she inquired sweetly. The john opened the door for the women.

As the car pulled away from the curb, Connie sat by the door, completely absorbed in her thoughts. After talking with the john for a few minutes, Vickie punched Connie in the ribs. "He wants to party with both of us, girl."

Connie grunted. "I don't feel like putting up with no goddamn trick," she stated, then went back into her own thoughts.

Vickie stared at her. She had never seen Connie like this. She began to talk quietly to the trick. The john stopped and parked on Wardwood in front of a large motel. Vickie twisted around in her seat and again approached her friend. "The man is willing to spend seventy-five dollars, Connie, if we both go with him. If you don't go, he'll only spend twenty-five dollars."

For a brief moment, the only sound that could be heard in the car was the heavy breathing of the john as he waited for the girls to make up their minds. Connie stared at the fat white man. His cheeks were heavy and hung in folds. All the heartbreak of the day arose in Connie's mind, and her hatred for the man became intense. She wanted to put her knife to his neck and just take his money. Connie could be ruthless whenever she took the notion. She was a large woman and also had a vile temper at times.

"What we goin' do, honey?" Vickie asked softly.

Without bothering to answer, Connie opened

the car door and got out. The john followed suit, leaving his car parked on the street. Vickie stared after the man and Connie, then shook her head and got out too. She followed the pair into the motel, where the john paid for a room, and they followed him down the hall with the clerk staring after them curiously.

The party hadn't taken long, but Vickie was shaken as she followed Connie and the trick back out of the motel. She had seen many things since becoming a prostitute, but today had really shocked her. She looked at the man and shivered. She knew that he was perverted, but she was still stunned—more by the way Connie had acted than by what he had asked for.

The man had wanted to be beaten while committing an act of oral copulation on Vickie. Connie had delivered the beating with more than enough emotion. She had whipped the trick with a belt the man had supplied. He had rolled off of Vickie, crying that it was enough, but she had continued to beat him until he fell on the floor. After that, she had made him take out his wallet, and she had removed another hundred dollars from it. When the trick started to complain, she had started to beat him again.

Vickie had separated them, leaving the john to moan on the floor. Now that it was over, the john rolled his eyes angrily at Connie. He opened his car door. "You black bitch," he screamed at her, leaving no doubt about which one he was talking to.

"Fuck you in your ass, you freakish bastard," Connie screamed after him, putting her hands on her hips and staring angrily at him. He slammed his car door and locked it.

Before anything else could be said between them, a police car pulled up and stopped. A big, blond-headed man snarled from the passenger seat, "What the hell's wrong with you, gal? You know I don't allow no whoring on this street when I'm on shift."

"You're wrong, Frazer," Connie answered, using the officer's name. "We're just trying to catch a cab."

Vickie watched as the trick pulled off, and she felt relieved. At least they wouldn't get charged with robbery. This feeling was short-lived, though, as the officer got out and ushered them into the car. After they got in the car, the cop drove around slowly. Vickie, under the impression they were going to jail, sat back quietly.

"How much money have you girls made so far?" the officer named Frazer asked.

Connie stared at him. Her mouth was drawn up in an angry snarl. "We ain't made a goddamn thing," she spat out at him in anger.

Frazer stared at her for a moment. With slow, deliberate motions, he instructed his young driver to pull up in an alley. They parked behind a run-down house. He turned around in his seat and stared at Vickie. "You'll do just fine," he said and wet his lips with anticipation. "Get the hell out," he said to Vickie, opening the car door from the inside.

Vickie looked around, dumbfounded. Connie spoke up harshly. "The dirty sonofabitch wants to fuck, Vickie, Either you give him some free pussy or he takes your ass to jail." She made the statement matter-of-factly, but her voice was full of emotion, showing that she didn't like the idea at all.

Vickie hesitated, then she accepted her fate with a shrug. It wouldn't take but a minute, she reasoned, and it beat the hell out of going to jail. She missed Doris, but she didn't miss her that much.

Connie turned her back on the young officer she was left in the car with. When he tried to make small conversation, she simply ignored him. After about fifteen minutes of that cold treatment, he was glad to see his partner coming back. He sat up straighter in the seat. Frazer opened the car door and got in, grinning.

"That was wonderful, boy," he said to his partner as he climbed in beside him.

Vickie opened the back door and started to get in beside Connie. Before she could close the door, Connie shoved her from the car, then climbed out.

"Where the hell do you think you're going?" Frazer asked sharply.

Connie put her hands on her hips. "You're finished with your fuckin' around, so now what you want us to do, grow old with you?"

Frazer glanced at his partner. "My friend here has some plans for you, Connie, so just hold your

horses."

Connie spit on top of the police car. "I'll tell you what you can do, Frazer. You take your partner and do whatever you think he wants me to do *for* me, honkie."

For a minute Frazer didn't understand, but then his face started to turn red and he opened the car door to get out. "Why, you black bitch!" he managed to say.

Connie's nose flared and she shook her fist at the officer. "I got your black bitch hanging," she said.

"Why," he sputtered, "I'll take your black ass to jail if you don't shut your fuckin' mouth!"

"If anybody should know how black it is, you should, you cunt-lapping bastard, you," she screamed in his enraged face. Vickie pulled her by the arm and dragged her away from the car.

Frazer was so mad he was choking on his words. If it hadn't been for that, Vickie wouldn't have been able to get her away. "Put that filthy whore in the car," he yelled at his partner. "Maybe after she gets downtown, she'll learn some fuckin' sense!"

Vickie pushed Connie towards an empty gangway that led towards the front of the street. "Run, honey, if you don't want to go to jail. I'll try and handle it for a minute."

Connie, realizing she had gone too far, pulled

her skirt up and ran. Vickie stopped the young officer, blocking the pathway with her body. "If you take us down, we goin' sure as hell tell it to the desk sergeant," she stated loudly, causing the officer to come to a complete stop.

Her words made him stop and think. He didn't want any blemish on his record, and something like this would never do. His young wife would have a fit if she heard about it—him playing around with whores. His hesitation was all they needed. Vickie caught up with Connie before she reached Earl's place, and the two women entered the apartment together.

Earl was sitting at the bar, drunk, staring foolishly at the empty glass he held in his hand. Connie grabbed him under the arms and got him to his feet. She waved Vickie away when Vickie offered to help. Without resisting, Earl staggered towards the bedroom. Connie entered behind him and slammed the door with her foot. She pushed Earl towards the bed, but he somehow missed the bed and fell, knocking over the night table and lamp.

He pushed the lamp out of his way and stared up at her, mad and half dazed. "Bitch! You losing your goddamn mind?" he asked harshly, not really knowing if it was her fault or his own. Drunk as he was, he realized she was angry, but she still had guidelines she had better respect. One thing disturbed him though. Every time they had fought, he had been sober. Connie was tall and solid, and he had to knock her out every time he had jumped on her in the past. The last thing he wanted in his present condition was a fight with her, so he decided to overlook what had happened.

"Doris got five years, nigger! Do you think you were worth five years out of her life?" The question jarred him halfway sober.

He shook his head to clear it up. He knew how much time Doris had gotten, so that was nothing new. His lawyer had called as soon as it happened. He remained silent and tried to get his wits together.

Ever since she had talked to Fay in the courtroom, Connie had been hurt and angry. Now it all came to a boiling point. She didn't care what Earl did. She stalked over to where he lay propped up against the bed on the floor. She stood over him and was tempted to kick him in the face. "I talked to Fay in the courtroom, Earl, and I wanted to kick the bitch's ass once we got outside, but she told me something that took all that desire away." She stared down at him and added, "It took the fire right out of me, mister."

Earl picked up a cigarette off the floor and felt around until he found a lighter. Connie studied him carefully before continuing. "I'm hoping that the bitch lied, Earl, but either way, man, I hope you'll tell me the truth." Her voice became shrill. "The bitch says you paid her a thousand dollars, Earl, one thousand dollars to drop the charges from you. Plus, you knew in advance that Doris' ass was in a world of trouble, 'cause she wasn't goin' drop the charges on both of you. Now, I want to know, man, if you went along with that cold shit?"

"So what if I *did* make a deal, bitch?" he asked, then regretted the words before they were out, wishing that he had lied instead, after he saw the expression on her face.

He tried to pull himself together, but the whiskey was controlling his actions.

Connie stepped nearer to Earl; her intent was plain. Earl managed to get up on the edge of the bed. "Bitch, if you do something crazy, I'll kick a mudhole in your ass," he stated coldly, gaining control of his senses.

She stopped and pointed a finger at him as though it were a gun. "You had the nerve to give that yellow bitch some of the money I been working day and night for, nigger?" Her voice was full of contempt. "I should bust you myself for pandering."

"Bitch," he yelled, and now his voice was full of emotion. "I don't know how drunk you think I am, but you get out of a whore's place and I'll break your goddamn neck!"

She leaned down and sneered. "Fuck you, nigger in your jive ass."

Earl moved quickly, but he was still under the influence of the whiskey. She sidestepped as he lunged at her, and she stuck out her foot as he went stumbling by, tripping him. He fell into the open closet, tearing some of his suits from their hangers as he reached out to break his fall.

Connie backed up towards the bedroom door. "If you put your hands on me, nigger, I'll scream and tear the roof off this joint," she said loudly as she fumbled for the doorknob.

"You better start screaming then, whore," Earl said as he climbed to his feet. A small trickle of blood ran down his face from a tiny gash where he had struck his head. "You better damn well know you're going to do some screaming, you crazy motherfucker," he yelled loudly.

Vickie burst through the open door and stepped between the fighting couple. She stared from one to the other with astonishment. Connie moved towards the vastness of the front room. She knew that Vickie wouldn't be able to stop Earl if he decided to fight, and she was pretty sure he was going to do some fighting—drunk or not. She realized just as quickly that she didn't have a chance of winning.

"You're a no-good, black motherfucker, Earl," she screamed as she reached the safety of the front door. She didn't think he could catch her in his condition. If things went hard, she reasoned, she could always take the stairway. And in his drunken condition, she didn't believe he could catch her on the stairway. As he staggered out of the bedroom, still in a sort of daze, she added, "And as long as I live, bastard, you're going to be a sack of cocksuckers, you foul motherfucker, you!"

Earl broke into a lumbering run. She darted out into the hallway. "Plus, you're a low-life bastard," she added, and slammed the door in his face when he reached it.

When he snatched open the door, she was already on the stairway, so he closed it and leaned against it. Yes, he had been right. It had turned out to be one hell of a day.

14

F AY STAGGERED AS SHE climbed from the bar stool. Her blonde wig had become incredibly dirty. It hung sideways in a funny slant on her head. Sister put both her elbows on the bar and stared at Fay. "I don't care what you say, Fay, when you was with Earl, you never allowed yourself to look like this."

Whenever she talked, Fay had adopted a way of holding her head sideways so that people couldn't see her disfigurement—or so she thought. The left side of her face was scarred, resembling a raw blister that looked as though it would never heal.

Fay staggered back from the bar and stood, spread legged. Her tall, slim build was still exciting to some men. "Don't mention that dirty sonofabitch to me," she cursed loudly, then staggered over to a table occupied by two white men. They glanced up at her coldly.

"What's wrong?" she asked drunkenly, "don't you guys want some company?" She tried to pull a chair out from under the table, but one of the men held it with his foot. The men ignored her and continued talking to each other.

She attempted to slam the chair against the table and stalk away angrily. Her temper was at the boiling point, and unconsciously she rubbed the scar on her face. She blamed Earl for all her troubles; as she staggered from the bar her hatred grew.

Across town, Vickie put the last of Earl's clothing in a suitcase. He had told her the cost of the penthouse was too much, so they had given it up. She had hated the thought of giving up the place, but Earl had been firm in his demand that they move to cheaper surroundings. A bellhop entered and removed the last bag almost before she had closed the latch on it.

Earl climbed down from the bar stool and glanced around for the last time. "Well, that about takes care of that."

"We didn't really have to move, Earl," she murmured. "This makes me feel like a sorry whore." Vickie stared down at the floor, embarrassed.

"Don't worry about it," he reassured her. "We been through all this shit before, baby. I done told you I want to grind up on a big bankroll." He smiled, then patted her on the behind. "After we get on full, Vickie, I'm taking you cross country, baby. Just you and me—and let you party a little bit. You know, show up the square bitches and all that shit. Just you and me, baby. This time next month, we should be on our way to California. "

She closed the door of the penthouse behind them and followed him towards the elevator. She had gotten over the heartache of leaving after listening to his words. "How much money do we have to have, daddy, before leaving?" she inquired gaily.

The elevator was empty, so Earl backed her up against the wall and held her tightly as he leaned against her. When they came to a stop at the lobby, he released her. Her eyes were bright and shining. "Don't let the money part disturb you, Vickie. I'll worry about that part. And when I think we are ready, I'll let you be the first to know, honey."

The very sound of his voice seemed to make sparks go off inside her. She knew she would do anything she possibly could to make that day come true, when just the two of them could ride off. How sweet it would be, she thought.

As they walked through the lobby, most of the men sitting there turned and watched them go out. More than one wished he could take Earl's place with such a lovely thing on his arm. She had that rare loveliness that only a few women in a generation possessed.

They took a small kitchenette apartment in the same building Earl had dealt in. Earl cut down on his champagne buying, and Vickie started to take bennies so that she could stay awake and work day and night. She was constantly in the streets, looking for the big one. Lately, however, no matter how hard she tried, her trap never exceeded two hundred a night. Earl had remarked rather coldly that it seemed that, after she got into the hundreds, she ran out of gas. What he had said, he had said off-handedly, not really paying attention and not really mad about the trap money. In fact, he was rather pleased with her efforts, but he hadn't taken the time to tell her that.

Vickie walked down the street, confused. What Earl had said hurt. It cut very deeply. She knew in her heart that he was wrong. She was trying, and she would go on trying. She wanted to take off a big one and give it to Earl—as big as, or bigger than, anything Connie had ever given him. She knew that, in the past, Connie had put her knife around a trick's neck and robbed him of a few grand, but she didn't know just how many thousand it had been. Robbery was something she had never tried, but if the opportunity ever presented itself, she believed that she was capable of doing it. Without thinking about it, she felt the knife in the top of her stocking and was reassured.

A car horn tooted, and she jumped back, surprised. "Damn," she swore quietly, smiling at the trick driving the car. Maybe Earl is right, she thought coldly. Here I am daydreaming and a trick damn near runs me over.

The small, wizened-faced man behind the steering wheel smiled timidly. Vickie opened the car door and slid in beside him. She studied her customer closely with an experienced eye. She noted that he was too small to be a policeman. When she had first started working, all white men looked alike to her. But it didn't take long for her to quickly learn her error. This one had a pale complexion with pockmarks covering most of his face. She noticed that he was nervous, so she smiled reassuringly at him. "You don't have to be shy, honey; I ain't goin' hurt you, baby."

"Ah ain't scared, gal," the trick answered, his voice a deep southern drawl.

Vickie pulled her skirt up higher and crossed her legs. "What's your name, honey?" she asked.

"Jimmy. That's what all my friends call me." His eyes darted down to her legs and became glued there for a moment. He had to snatch the steering wheel to avoid hitting a parked car.

"Be careful, honey," she said, pulling her skirt back down so that he could keep his attention on his driving. "Why don't we just park somewhere, baby, until we get some kind of understanding— cash understanding," she added.

Jimmy removed a wallet from his coat pocket and tossed it down between her legs. "I reckon you'll find enough darn money in that wallet, gal, for even *you*," he said as he turned a corner and pulled into an alley.

For a moment Vickie couldn't believe it. She stared at the contents of the wallet. It was crammed with money. She counted part of it, then twisted around and looked at the trick. He had been watching her out of the corner of his eye, but when he saw her looking, he glanced away.

Then for the first time she noticed she was in an alley. She sat up straighter, glancing around to get her bearings. She turned back towards the driver, who was so engrossed in trying to find a dark area to park that he wasn't paying much attention to her. She removed most of the money and stuck it in her bra, all the time watching him to see how he would react. She tried the door handle, but the car was moving too fast, and there was too much glass in the alley to take the chance of jumping. She decided to wait until a better opportunity came along.

He pulled in behind a hotel, beside a panel truck. Vickie recognized the rear of the hotel as the one that she lived in, so she relaxed as the thought flashed through her mind that she wouldn't have far to run. She held his wallet out to him, but he just took it out of her hand and tossed it on top of his dashboard. With one quick motion, she hit the door with her shoulder and the door handle with her hand, but the trick moved faster.

"Where the hell you think you goin', gal?" Jimmy said as he grabbed her arm and pulled her across the car seat. "Here you done stole most of my money, whore, now you want to run off."

Her head struck the steering wheel as he brutally shoved her down on the car seat. "Take it easy, honey," she sad as the john ripped at her clothing. "Just take your time. I'm going to do what you want, but I don't want my clothes torn."

The trick was beyond control now. She stared up into his eyes and a shiver of fear ran down her spine. She had never seen madness before in a man's eyes, but she knew at once what it was when she saw it.

"Fuck that! Fuck that! Fuck that!" he yelled, making a song out of the words. He continued to spill filth from his mouth as he ripped at her clothes. He wouldn't allow her the time to take them off herself.

He yanked at the yellow sweater she wore and the buttons broke as he ripped it open. Suddenly pain burst out all over her chest as he dropped his head on her breast. He lifted his head for a moment, and she could see parts of her blouse and bra in his mouth. He spit the cloth from his mouth and stared madly at her now-exposed breasts.

"Yes, yes, yes, yes, yes," he said rapidly, "these will do just fine, just fine." He glared down at her wildly, then cautioned, "Don't scream, now. Don't scream, don't scream." He repeated it over and over, then dropped his head to her breast again.

She had an idea of what was coming from his earlier attempt, so this time she tried desperately to keep his mouth away from her breasts. With all her strength, she tried to hold him back, but he was just as determined to reach them. Pain, pain that she had never imagined could exist, exploded in her chest, and she could feel his teeth penetrate her breast.

Furiously, she screamed. Scream after scream. She was frightened, hurt, and enraged. Her right leg was pinned to the front seat, but she fumbled desperately with the top of her stockings as she searched for her knife. What she had always visualized was finally coming true—getting jammed up with a nut.

"Ah done told you, gal, about that hollerin'," he said, his face looming above hers. Blood, her blood, dropped down into her face from his yellow teeth. As she stared up at him, she almost fainted. Her nipple was hanging from his mouth. He chewed on it like bubble gum.

The sight of part of her in his mouth only intensified her struggle. She finally managed to reach her knife, but it was too late. A long butcher knife flashed in his hand. He had hidden it beneath the driver's seat.

With all her remaining strength, she twisted and tossed him against the dashboard as she fumbled to pop her knife open. As she opened the weapon, she tried to block the butcher knife, which he had plunged at her viciously. She partially blocked his aim, but the butcher knife fell with deadly precision. He struck straight into the open wound on her chest and, reaching down, he fumbled for his penis, then slid down between her legs with it in his other hand.

The pain was unbearable, but she managed to raise the knife upward, and as he fell on her, he impaled himself. She prayed for strength and pushed the knife upward in his chest as his scream shook the car. "Not yet, motherfucker," she murmured unconsciously to herself. Her motions now were those of a sleepwalker. She didn't know what she was doing. As he tried to pull away from her, she came upward and outward with the knife, delivering a stroke just as deadly as the one he had given her.

The car door flew open and two black hands reached in and jerked the white man violently from her. There was wild cursing going on in the background, but she couldn't seem to understand why. The pain in her breast wouldn't go away, and she had the sensation of people staring in the car at her. She felt more than saw someone reach in and pull her skirt down gently. She tried to straighten out her legs, but she couldn't feel anything. Blackness seemed to overcome her, and she slipped off into the void.

* * *

Inside the bar, the air conditioner had made it quite comfortable for the people relaxing there. Earl twirled the drink in his glass around and around. Mrs. Jones peeped into the bar. She saw Earl and approached him, bending down to whisper hurriedly in his ear. His eyes became wider as he talked, and suddenly he jumped from the stool and rushed from the bar. The other customers stared at him curiously, wondering why he was rushing on such a hot day.

Earl came out of the rear of the hotel and stopped. He noticed a white man lying on the ground holding his stomach and moaning. Relief flooded through him. The old bitch had it wrong, he thought quickly. What she had probably meant was that Vickie had fucked up and stabbed a trick. Damn, he cursed, this was going to cost him a lot of money, but he had to keep her out of jail. It was unbearable to even think about her being gone for a few days, let alone off on a manslaughter charge. He'd just have to leave town with her in a hurry, he reasoned, as his eyes took in the crowd of curious people.

A tall, dark-complexioned boy yelled. "Over here, Earl, she's in the car!"

His words were like a bombshell. Earl moved towards the car like a sleepwalker, not knowing what to expect, but really not expecting what awaited him. The few people standing in his way stepped back, allowing him to approach the car.

Earl opened the passenger door and caught his

breath. He slipped to the floor beside her, picking up her head gently. "Oh, my god," he moaned tearfully. As he cradled her in his arms, his eyes took in her mutilated body. Tears gushed from his eyes and mingled with the blood that ran freely from her breast. She lay in his arms, motionless. Her eyes fluttered open, and the vacant stare disappeared. She recognized him. "Oh, daddy," she managed to say. "I knew I'd get a big one for you, honey." She raised her left hand. Clutched in her fist was a roll of blood-soaked money. She managed to push the money into his open coat pocket, then her hand fell to the seat. "A big one, daddy," she mumbled before her eyes went glassy. Life vanished from her like a puff of smoke.

Earl cried as he gently closed her eyes. He had seen too much death in the ghetto not to be able to recognize it—even if he didn't want to accept it. The tears fell slowly as he moved like a man in a trance.

The sound of a siren wrenched him from his zombie-like state. He placed her gently on the car seat and climbed out. The powder-blue suit he wore was ruined. Large splotches of blood were his reminder of their last embrace. Earl stopped beside the body of Jimmy. Vickie's knife still protruded from his body as evidence of the terrible fight. A red, revealing line around his mouth brought to view his vicious crime even while death claimed his sickened soul.

Turning away in disgust, Earl staggered, tears

blinding him. Ike, the young man who had waved Earl towards the car, stopped and put his arm around Earl's shoulder. "Now's the time, big feller, for you to show strength," he said. "All you got to do is hold on, man, just hold on."

"It's funny," Earl said in a broken voice, "how things like this can happen out of a clear sky. We were just about to get over and ride out, and then this shit happened."

Ike nodded as he removed a newspaper from under his arm. He revealed the headlines:

KILLER ESCAPES FROM MENTAL HOSPITAL

Earl looked away as Ike read the small print. "He done killed four other women, Earl." He pointed out Jimmy's picture at the bottom of the page. "It says here, Earl, that he stole two thousand dollars from the hospital. That must have been the money Vickie was holding so tight." His words caused Earl to glance up. "I could have took the money from her, Earl, but I knowed it would have killed her, so I left it for you."

"Thanks, Ike. Give me a chance to get my mind together, then I'll take care of you."

A police car pulled into the alley with its tires screaming. Both men walked towards the building. "How about doing me another favor, Ike?" Earl asked quietly.

"Of course, brother," Ike answered. "All you got to do is ask, man, that's all."

"Come on, then," Earl said as he opened the door. "Ain't no sense us getting involved in the police work. Looks like they gettin' ready to start asking for names, and I don't want none of that shit."

They stepped briskly up the stairway of the hotel. A large crowd had gathered, so the police didn't notice their departure.

"I want you to rent me another room on the second floor, Ike. Get it under the name of Dickens—John Dickens." Earl's mind was moving again, and now he was trying to stay a move ahead of the police. "Hurry now, Ike; one of them squares out there will be done got some cop's ear, man, and they goin' come lookin' for this money."

Ike agreed. He knew how true-blue citizens reacted. They might get their pictures in the paper, so they hoped. He ran down the stairs, not wanting to lose out on his share of the money.

Once inside the apartment, Earl hurriedly started to pack, without bothering to change clothes. By the time Ike knocked on the door, he was fastening the last clasp on his suitcase. He had decided to leave most of her clothes. He only took her mink and her diamond ring and watch. Ike's knock scared him so badly that he almost refused to open the door.

"It's me, baby," Ike yelled from the hallway. "Open up, man! We got to move!"

Earl picked up an armload of suits he hadn't bothered to pack and carried them to the door. He shoved them into Ike's open arms. "What's the room number, baby?" he asked.

"You got room eighteen, man," Ike replied as he staggered down the hall with his load. Earl rushed back and grabbed the three pieces of luggage. He shoved them out into the hallway, then glanced around the now-empty apartment. The stuff that he had to leave could be easily replaced. His main concern now was to stay in front of the police. Earl glanced quickly at his watch. Everything that had happened had occurred in the past thirty minutes. His small world had crumbled around him in that short time.

When he reached the new apartment, he sat down on the bed and held his head. It was hard to believe things had happened so fast. Ike fidgeted restlessly. Too much had happened to him tonight for him to be quiet. His voice was low at first, but it grew stronger as he talked.

"I was the first one on the scene, man. You know, my room is right on the back there," he explained and stared at the silent Earl before continuing. "I hear this car pull up, you know, so I opens my shade and turns the lights out. I do this, Earl, just in case some trick should park and lock his wallet up in the car—you understand. I don't want to miss no sure shot, or have him sending the police up to my place either, if he sees me. I'd make a sorry witness if someone beat him for his wallet, but I don't want this problem." He shrugged his shoulders, then continued. "Ain't no sense me having no trouble. Anyway, I see the car pull up. It don't take but a second for me to figure somebody's woman done copped a trick. So I start watching to see if the trick hides his money, when all of a sudden they start acting up in the front seat. I figure whoever the girl is, she must have tried beatin' the trick in the car, instead of waitin' until they got in the hotel. Maybe she figured it was faster that way."

Ike glanced down at the floor, then lit a cigarette. "From where I was at, it looked like the girl opened the car door 'cause the light came on, and I recognized Vickie. I knew then that the john was gettin' ripped off, but the door slammed shut before she could get out, and I really started watching." Unknowingly, tears began to gather in Ike's eyes. To him, Vickie had been all he would have ever wanted in a woman. He was a young boy to most of the girls who worked in and out of the bar, and he didn't have a girl yet, so most of them—many of them younger than he ignored him. Vickie had always had a kind word for him; she treated him like a man, and he daydreamed about her. When she sat in the bar and drank a Coke with him, this made him happy. He was young, lonely, and on his own.

He continued, "I don't know what happened. They seemed to start struggling, but they both went down out of sight, and the only thing I can see is Vickie's foot come up on the dash, so I think they're taking care of business in the car. Suddenly I hear a scream. The trick's head pops up and I don't know what's happening." Ike tossed his arms up in disgust. Earl stared at him and saw tears running down his cheeks. "At first, I don't know who yelled," he continued, "Vickie or the trick. Then the trick drops down out of sight again. Now I really start hearing some screams. I jump up and grab my pants, figuring the trick done caught her dippin' and he's chokin' her or something." He pointed down at the slippers he wore. "I didn't stop, man, until I was outside beside the car. This is when I see the butcher knife in his hand. I still thought I was in time." He shook his head in horror. "Earl, I swear to god, and my mother dies if I'm lying, I snatched that honkey off Vickie so hard, I damn near broke his fuckin' neck."

Both men became silent, filled with their bitter thoughts, then Ike broke the silence, his voice still filled with emotion. "After I saw what that nut had did, I took my foot and pushed Vickie's knife down into him to the hilt. When the blood began to run out of his mouth, I left him alone."

His admission of guilt meant nothing to Earl. By rights, he could be booked on an open charge of murder, but that was the last thing on Earl's mind. His words had painted a picture so vivid that Earl stuck his face in a pillow to hide his grief. Every now and then a muffled sob could be heard. He remained quiet in his grief, but his back would rise and fall as heavy sobs escaped his lips.

Ike got up and left. He had witnessed things that would remain in his mind until his death. He went to the bar and returned carrying two pints of whiskey. He set them inside the room without speaking. Earl had not moved since he left, so he departed, quite shaken by Earl's sincere grief.

That night, Ike sat in his room in the dark. Many things crossed his mind. He knew that many pimps thought less of their women than they did of the cars they drove. When he talked to them, they were quick to say that a whore *fell* in love, a pimp *made* love. He didn't know if this was true or not, because he had never had a whore, but he was sure of one thing: the pimp upstairs had let the game turn him around. Earl had fallen in love; of this he was sure, 'cause no man could cry that hard over something he didn't care about.

15

THE FUNERAL WAS WHAT one would call a crowded affair. Earl watched from a darkened doorway across the street from the funeral parlor. He knew the police would be there, waiting and watching for him, and he had no desire to answer their probing questions.

When the casket came out, the people flowed out of the building behind it. They poured into the street to fill the waiting cars. Cadillacs stood bumper to bumper as all the nightlife crowd turned out to show their respect. Earl had to walk for almost two blocks to find Billy's Cadillac parked at the end of the funeral procession. Billy arrived soon after with his lady, Sandra, in tow. The frail, dark-complexioned prostitute had been crying; her eyes were red.

"I wondered where you were hiding, Earl," Billy said as he slid under the steering wheel.

It took half an hour before the long funeral could get underway. The three rode in silence until Sandra finally said, "That preacher sure had a lot to say. He preached a good sermon of her."

Billy snorted and poured a paper cup full of whiskey. He passed the drink over the seat to Earl, then poured himself one. "The only thing I could find wrong with the fuckin' preacher was the fact that the bastard talked too goddamn much."

"You nigger men!" Sandra said, disgustedly. "You're really something else. Maybe he didn't have to say nothing about her workin' the streets, but the rest of the stuff he preached was all right."

The procession moved slowly. Billy managed to get his Cadillac in behind Carl's. "That crap that preacher said about hustling don't mean shit!" he remarked. "Half the fuckin' church was full of whores, and the other half was full of pimps."

"How did her mother take it?" Earl asked quietly, his mood still somber.

Billy laughed coldly. "Right on cue. She performed, the pretending bitch. Whenever the preacher lightened up to catch his wind, she would fill in the slack. For a minute there, I thought maybe her and the preacher had a thing going on."

"I told you," Sandra stated loudly, "you niggers ain't shit. I can't understand why a whore would want to give one of you her money." She turned her back and stared out of the window as if she weren't a whore.

"After they get her in the ground, Earl, every- body that's cool is meeting over to Carl's," Billy said, then added, "That's the last party for the departed. We party all night, then in the morning everybody keeps right on steppin'."

"Keep on steppin'," Earl repeated. The phrase stuck with him. For the past three days all he had managed to do was stay drunk. Ike, Carl—even dope-fiend Pat—they all had stopped by and told him the same thing: keep on steppin'. He knew he had to do something. He couldn't keep on going the way he'd been traveling—drinking all night until he fell across his bed in the mornings, dead drunk.

The stop at the cemetery turned out to be a very sad affair indeed. It was heartbreaking. Most of the prostitutes who gathered there broke down and cried loudly. They felt fear for the unknown. This was a danger that moved close to their lives. Their friend and companion had been trapped by this vile evil. Each one promised herself that she would check her tricks more closely, and for the next week, every pimp with a girl in the streets would end up with short money as the fear continued to feed on their minds.

Earl stayed in the car just to avoid running into Vickie's mother. He could see them lowering the casket into the ground. His chest exploded with pain. He rolled on the seat and fought to catch his breath. Deep painful sobs choked him as they caught in his throat. He cried as no man wished to cry. He wondered how he could exist without her love. The very thought of going back to his empty hotel room filled him with fear of the loneliness that awaited him.

Sandra opened the car door and climbed into the back. She removed his tie for him so that he could breathe better. He started to tell her that nothing would help, or could help. Billy watched as his woman tried to help Earl. He understood. He didn't think that he would break down if his woman died, but it brought tears to his eyes to watch them lower Vickie's casket into the ground and to realize that all that young life was gone. He felt truly sorry for Earl, as he looked away.

Earl tried to straighten up. He didn't want anyone to see his grief. "It's all right," he managed to say. "I can handle it."

Sandra climbed back in the front and they drove slowly out of the cemetery. The ride back to the city was much faster than when they came out. Billy followed Carl back. Every time he looked in his mirror, he would see a line of Caddies in behind him.

Carl's party started slowly. The memory of death still lingered. Whiskey soon loosened everyone up, and they started swinging full blast. Around four in the morning, everyone was drunk, and half of them had forgotten what the party was for. Couples began to drift out heading for their favorite motels.

"Fuck it, fuck it," Earl murmured as he staggered down the bar and sat down at a table with Pat and Carl. Charles and Tammy moved closer. Billy and Sandra got behind the bar and set out fresh drinks for everyone.

Duke walked behind the bar and poured a water glass full of whiskey. He held the glass high for all to see. "I am not the host, but I say, let's have a toast." He glanced up and down the bar. Everyone lifted glasses in response:

"This is to a brown-skilled moll,
Who looked like a China doll,
When she worked on the street of sin.
Up and down she'd prod,
With a wink and a nod,
As she'd steer a trick
To the nearest whorehouse den."

Glasses were emptied, and Sandra quickly refilled them. Carl grabbed the water glass and held it high. Silence fell as he took up where Duke had left off:

"She was a top-notch broad,
A pro and a fraud,
And stuff
She played like a vet.

Why, many a man,
That we all know can,
Refused to lay her a bet."

Charles dropped his head to the bar, knocking over a glass. "I'm sure glad I ain't got to drive," he mumbled, "'cause if ya keep drinking every time somebody toasts, somebody goin' get too drunk to go home." He pointed at the water glass. "Fill it up for me, Sandra." He waited until she brought him the drink, then raised the glass unsteadily, and began:

"Here's to a good whore
That we all used to know.
We sent her away in style.
So when I go
Through that same door,
Line the Caddies
Up for a mile."

Pat laughed loudly and drained her glass. "That's all you pimps care about: pockets full of money to blow and a Cadillac." She pointed towards the water glass:

"Now I'm making a toast,
And it's not a boast,
I'm a dope fiend
As we all know.
But I would've gave up

My stuff,
If it had been enough,
To prevent such a blow."

"Duke," Billy yelled drunkenly. "I don't know why you started this shit. Last time we did it at Farrow's wake, damn near everybody ended up falling out." Ignoring his own prediction, Billy filled the water glass, which was gaily accepted as the speaker's drinking glass. If you couldn't handle a water glass full of whiskey, you couldn't take your turn as a toaster. Billy slammed the glass down with a bang and began:

"How she would follow
The almighty dollar.
In Hell she would even explore,
And sit there waitin'
To trick with ol' Satan.
Now *that* was a money-makin' whore!"

Sandra took her turn quickly. She was basically a deep-rooted religious woman. Actually, she would have felt better saying a prayer, but instead she said a toast:

"The jungle creed
Says the strong must feed
On any prey at hand.
So branded as beast,
Vickie sat down at feast,

And learned that her prey
Was man."

A few of the lesser-known young pimps sat around at the tables with their ladies. They knew that they would be out of place if they reached for the water glass, so they watched and listened in silence. One of Carl's barmaids kept the tables well supplied with fresh drinks.

Charles twisted around and stared at his woman. Tammy shook her head, declining. She had only met Vickie twice, and she didn't know what to say. This was the first time she had ever seen anyone do this after a funeral.

Nobody asked for the glass. Billy refilled it and faced the crowd, holding the glass outward. He slowly turned towards Earl and slammed the glass down in front of him. Everyone's eyes followed the move.

Earl's voice was low as he spoke, causing everyone to lean forward in an attempt to catch his words. "Anything I say will be inadequate. But I will try, inept as I am," he stated, as he slowly ran his fingers around the glass:

"There was no track
Known to be too fast
For this lady of the night.
Nor was there a whore,
Who could sting for more
Than Vickie—when her fingers

Were right.
Sun, snow, or hail
To her were the same.
Even the jail
She called part of the game.
And here we all sit
With tears in our eyes,
Desperately trying to
Say our goodbyes.
But if Vickie were here,
She'd say,
'Dry up those tears!
For another good whore's
Gone to *meet* all her peers.' "

Earl drained the glass and shattered it against the wall. "That's one I owe you, Carl," he said and staggered out the door.

16

THE NEXT FEW WEEKS passed slowly and uneventfully for Earl. His bankroll was dwindling and nothing was coming in. As he drove slowly down the street, he decided to stop and check out a young girl he had been wasting some time on. He pulled in front of a restaurant that he had begun patronizing and parked. He stared at the door to the place with indecision. He knew that he needed fresh money, and the waitress he was talking to didn't believe in giving up any money. Not yet, he reminded himself as he got out.

He entered and walked over to a table. The restaurant was small but neat. Its biggest clientele seemed to be the high-school kids that came by daily. A young girl about fifteen dropped some change in the jukebox, and the latest soul tune came screaming out. She danced across the floor, stopped, and winked at Earl, then continued on to her table and friends.

Earl ignored her and beckoned for the waitress. She came on the run, twisting between the tables quickly. She smiled gaily at Earl. "Hi, honey," she said cheerfully as she reached his table.

Slowly, with a measured gesture, he removed a cigarette pack from his inside pocket. He had started taking an interest in his appearance again. The dark-green silk suit he wore made him look like a male model.

The waitress giggled foolishly as she searched for a match. Earl waited patiently. His eyes boldly ran up and down her tight-fitting work dress. He studied her large legs so openly she blushed.

"Earl, don't look at me like that," she managed to say as she lit a match and leaned over. He ignored the burning match and stared down into her open blouse. The match burned her finger and she dropped it with a little squeal.

He broke into laughter and used his cigarette lighter. His voice dropped to a bedroom whisper, "Don't look at you *how*, Brenda?"

Brenda was five foot, with no inches to spare. Earl could just stare at her a certain way and she would blush. He stared at her again, and she turned scarlet red.

He reached out and grabbed her arm. "Please, Earl, please!" she begged, while glancing around to see who was watching. She twisted back and slapped his hand. "Stop, Earl; don't do that."

"I know you like it, girl. You ain't got to put on with me," he said quietly.

Her ears turned scarlet and she backed away from his intimate caress. "What you want, man? I ain't got time to play."

Earl became serious. "Since you think I'm playing, send the other waitress over."

Brenda studied him closely to see if he was serious. She didn't want the other girl to wait on Earl. She stepped back to the table and leaned against his arm. "What you want, huh?"

"I want some money, baby, cash," Earl said lightly.

Brenda laughed and put one hand on her hip. She was short but stacked. Everything was large for her size. She'd turn to fat later in life, Earl thought. "All the money you carry around, Earl, I know you don't really need any of the small change I make. You drive a big Cadillac and wear almost as many diamonds as you want to."

It was his turn to study her. He wondered momentarily if she was trying to be funny. The bitch is either dumb or not wrapped too tight, he thought. "Listen, Brenda, I'm talking about *your* money, baby. You know you need a manager."

She looked down at the floor. "The other girls told me you was a pimp, Earl. Is that what you are?"

"The only thing you have to concern yourself about, girl, is the fact that I'm a man and you getting your action." Earl puffed on his cigarette for a brief moment, then added, "I don't want to hear nothing about what somebody told you. I need some money, and I want you to have me some."

She looked around nervously. "I don't get paid until Thursday, Earl," she blushed, then looked away and added, "You can have all of it except ten dollars, if you need it."

He asked curiously, "What you need with ten dollars? Your mother takes care of you, don't she?"

"I have to pay rent at home, but I'll give you the rest of it," she said quietly.

Earl pushed the chair back and got up. He grabbed her in his arms before she could get away. The proprietor shook his head and Earl released her. "I'll pick you up Thursday night." He bent and whispered in her ear. "I might bust that cherry for you." He raised his voice. "Be ready to give it up, baby."

"Earl," she uttered, then blushed a deep pink. She turned and fled towards the counter with Earl's laughter ringing in her ears.

He walked out of the place smiling. It wasn't every day that he got a chance to pluck off a virgin and a paycheck too. He glanced at his watch. Billy had called that morning and set up an appointment. It had to be important because Billy wouldn't talk over the phone. That was a hell of a thing, he reasoned. People taking care of business these days wouldn't dare talk about it over the phone, if they had any sense.

Earl reached the meeting place three minutes early. He drove past and went around the block before making a U-turn. He drove slowly on the way back, catching a light on purpose. He checked his watch: one minute to go. The light changed and he eased down on the gas pedal. When he reached the meeting place, he drove right up into the gas station.

Billy was already there. The attendant was checking under his hood. Earl stopped at a pump and got out. Neither man greeted the other. Billy walked over towards the Coke machine. Earl looked around casually before walking towards the machine. Billy held a quarter towards the approaching Earl.

"You got change, buddy?" he asked loudly.

Removing a handful of change, Earl answered, "A pocketful, mister. What you want?"

Billy put a dime into the machine and got a Coke. "Big things going down tonight," he said quietly. "If you got some money, you can get down with me, Earl, and make yourself four times what your roll is now."

Earl put his hand into the machine and got out his Coke. "How much time have I got before you get down, man?"

The gas station attendant closed Billy's hood and walked around to the back of the car. "I'll be at your place for the money in two hours. How much money, Earl, are you goin' get down with?"

Donald Goines

Earl hesitated for a moment. "Put me down for two grand, Billy." Billy nodded and went back towards his car.

Earl drove slowly on the way back to the heart of the city. He parked in front of a pawn shop. It's a pity, he reasoned, but it was the only way out of his tight. The diamonds had to go.

17

AFTER ARRIVING ON SCHEDULE, Billy picked up the money and departed. He carried the giant bankroll in a briefcase. Seeing all the money Billy had stuffed into the briefcase made Earl relax a little about the investment. He tried not to worry, but it was his last money and, for some reason, uneasiness rode with him. He glanced at his arm for the time of day, and cursed when he realized that he had had to pawn his watch. He had to call the desk to get the time, and that didn't help his temper.

Earl ordered a pint of whiskey from the bar. The night went by slowly. It didn't take this long to grow dope, he thought. He began to wish he hadn't got down on this one—wished that he hadn't been so impulsive. Again he wished he hadn't pawned his diamonds.

Somebody knocked hard on his door. Earl jumped to his feet and rushed to the door. Carl grinned. "What's going on, man; you letting friends in tonight?"

Earl stepped back to let him enter. Carl waited until Earl had closed the door and asked, "Have you heard from Billy yet?"

Earl shook his head. "Is that what got you so nervous, Carl?"

Carl paced up and down the room. "I got five thousand dollars out in the wind, man. Don't you think that's enough to be sweating about?"

"Yeah, baby," Earl agreed readily. "I ain't got that much tied up, but what's out in the wind, man, is sure nuff my very goddamn last." He flashed his wrist.

Dropping down in a chair, Carl replied, "You know damn well that wasn't your last money, Earl."

Earl waved his arm to display its nakedness. "You think I'd pawn my shit if I had some cash, man?"

Carl changed the sensitive subject. "How have the whores been treating you, baby?"

This was even more sensitive and caused Earl to snap, "You keep your goddamn ear to the ground, Carl. You know as well as I do that, whenever a new whore shows up, that funky bitch Fay puts mud all over my name or scares. the bitch some kind of fuckin' way!"

Carl shrugged. "I've heard that crap she supposed to be telling all the young whores, but I know you ain't letting that junk hold you back."

"It don't," Earl admitted. "It's just that good whores don't grow on trees. If they were that easy to get, everybody would have one or two."

Carl nodded in agreement. The two men sat sipping their whiskey and whiled the slow-moving night away by discussing various ladies of the night.

After leaving Earl, Billy had Duke drive him straight across town. He parked down the street from an expensive hotel. "You sure you don't want me to go inside with you, Billy? That's a hell of a lot of money you're carrying, man."

Billy looked at his friend. "Naw, Duke, it ain't necessary. These are white boys I'm doing business with."

"When it comes to twenty-five thousand dollars, Billy, it don't make no difference. White boys, black boys—either would kill Jesus for that kind of cash, baby."

"Don't worry," Billy said, punching him lightly on the arm. "Big boys, Duke, always respect each other."

Duke pulled his coat back and removed a snub-nosed thirty-eight. "Take this with you. This is something else the big guys respect, too."

Billy took both gun and holster and jammed them down into his belt. A little insurance never hurt, he reasoned. It had been his intention to get the pistol from Duke before he left the car, but he didn't mention this fact to his close friend.

"I'm glad you're lookin' out for me, mellow," Billy said with a grin, opening the car door.

Duke started to ask again but stopped.

"Don't worry," Billy remarked, seeing the look of concern on his friend's face. He leaned down to the car window and covered up the butt of the gun. "These white boys don't know what's happening, man. With our outlet, Duke, we might tear off close to three hundred thousand, boy." He winked, and Duke watched him walk away.

Billy stopped as he started to depart from the elevator and allowed an elderly, mink-coated lady with her poodle to go first.

She smiled her thanks to the neatly dressed Negro male. He's attractive, even though he's dark, she thought, and continued down the hall.

Billy stopped at the first door on his right and knocked. He had called up from the lobby, but they still opened the door on a chain. An eye peeped out, studied Billy carefully, then the door opened and he stepped into the room. A tall, dark-complexioned Italian greeted him. "Billy boy, I'm really glad to see you. Looks like you're gaining weight around the middle," he said, looking at the bulge the thirty-eight made.

"Well, Tony, you know how this business goes. That's one place you better gain some weight at."

Tony sneered. He pulled his coat open. "You

see how clean I am? It's just a way to show that I
think I'm doing business with my friends."

Billy jerked his head at the doorman. "I guess
he's just as clean."

Tony looked annoyed. "You got to trust somebody, man."

"I do," Billy answered flatly. He tossed his briefcase on the table. "Let's get down to business; I
got people waiting."

Tony opened the briefcase, and Billy stuck out
his hand, stopping him from dumping the money
out on the table.

"I come to do business, Tony, not bullshit. Let
me see some dope." Neither man really trusted
the other, and they eyed each other with hostility.
Billy removed a small paper bag from his pocket.
"What's that you got there?" Tony asked curiously.

"It's mix, for the dope, if you ever come up
with some."

Tony shook his head. "I don't know if we got
time for all that crap."

"My money spends anywhere, Tony. You got
time to do everything else. I know you can find
time for me to check what I'm buying." Billy measured eight small amounts out on the table, like
eight separate ant hills. "You said it would take
ten cuts, Tony. I'm not going to put but eight on
it. If it takes that, I'll be happy."

Tony pulled a package from his pocket. "This
dope here will take eight, plus some," he said,
tossing the package on the table.

Billy examined the small pack closely. "I'm supposed to be getting two kilos of stuff, man. Twelve thousand five hundred a pack."

Another pack fell on the table. "You can't test but one at a time, can you?"

Billy picked up the last pack. "I don't have to test but one." He quickly made a small hole in the package. With deft motions, he filled a spoon with dope and smoothed it out. He produced a small strainer and dropped dope and mix into it together. He slowly sprinkled the mixture back onto the table.

Someone knocked on the door lightly. Billy glanced up, annoyed. "What the fuck's happening?" he asked sharply.

"It's Mike," the doorman yelled. Tony took a peek at Billy, then said, "Let him in. He's all right."

Billy had to hold himself in check. He didn't like it, but it wasn't his place to complain. His anger quickly grew to alarm. The man called Mike entered, followed closely by two large, hard-faced men. "What the fuck's going on here, Tony?" Billy asked sharply. The words were hardly out of his mouth before the three men produced pistols.

Mike stepped forward. "Just keep your mouth shut, boy, and everything will be all right." He waved his gun in Billy's direction. "That way, nigger, you might live to tell somebody what happened."

Billy glanced around, bewildered. All the money he had collected from the different people was not

Tony's concern; it was his alone. They would never believe he got ripped off. Plus, all the money he had saved for the past year was tied up in this deal. He analyzed the situation quickly, and his anger overrode his caution.

"You sonofabitch!" he said to Tony. "Don't think I'm goin' buy this shit or accept it!"

Tony gestured helplessness with his hands. "I ain't got nothing to do with this, Billy. You gotta believe me, man."

Mike pushed his gun under Billy's nose and picked up the briefcase. He then reached across the table and picked up the package of dope.

Billy's eyes had become mere slits as he stared at Tony. "I ain't the one who has to believe this shit, Tony. I'm calling New York, mister, and we'll see if the big man believes you."

Tony turned pale and his hands started to shake. Mike silently began to screw on a silencer to his pistol.

Billy's eyes opened wide in horror. He stared at the silencer as though he couldn't believe what he saw. He had never been a coward, and now, knowing that he was about to die, he gambled everything. Desperately he made his move. Pushing the table towards Mike, he reached for his gun. Pain exploded in his chest and Billy fell to the floor, his gun still tucked into his waistband.

Tony stared down at the Negro on the floor. Awareness of what had happened, or what he had allowed to happen, came to him in a rush. Billy had been well thought of by the Bossman. His anger turned towards Mike. "What the hell ever made you go and kill him for?" he yelled. "There wasn't no killing mentioned in the deal."

Mike shrugged his wide shoulders. He was tall and lean, with pale blue eyes. "That boy was going to cause us a lot of trouble, Tony, about the money."

"But murder?" Tony managed to sputter. His eyes followed the pistol that Mike raised and pointed directly at his stomach.

"I understand what you mean, Mike," Tony muttered as he stared at the gun. "I understand now. We couldn't have done it any other way, Mike. And besides, who gives a damn about a nigger?" He tried to grin and laugh it off.

Mike stared without blinking. His eyes held the same coldness that a reptile's eyes would have. "I figured you would understand, Tony," he said, and he pulled the trigger.

Tony staggered back, holding his hands to his stomach. There was fear in his dark eyes as he stared around the room in helpless pain. "Help me, somebody," he begged as the gun spit fire again.

The doorman backed up towards the door. "You know me, Mike; I'm with you guys all the way."

Mike nodded in agreement. "I know you are, boy. Don't worry about a thing."

One of Mike's henchmen stepped from the restroom. He had screwed on a silencer, too. He waited for Mike to give him the go-ahead. Mike nodded. The gun in the man's hand spit fire and the doorman fell against the wall, then slid down on the floor. The gunman walked over and put the gun against his head and pulled the trigger again.

As Mike started for the door with the briefcase under his arm, the phone rang. "Maybe one of them guys will answer it," he said laughingly as he closed the door to the apartment and walked quickly down the hall.

Inside the room, Tony rolled over and reached for the cord. The phone rang shrilly in his ear. He pulled the cord and the phone came tumbling down to the floor. He grabbed the receiver and clutched it firmly. "What's going on over there?" a strong voice asked.

"Boss," he managed to mutter, "get Mike, Mike Nelson." The phone slipped from his grasp. On the other end of the line, a man held the receiver and listened silently. He pointed his finger at two young men sitting in his office.

"Catch a plane. Get over there and see what's happened." He fell silent for a second, then added, "It just might be a small problem came up. Find out where Mike Nelson's holed up. It's just possible he might have stepped out of line. If so, I want you to hang that blue-eyed bastard's ass up to dry."

18

THE DOOR BANGED AS though someone were trying to break it down. Earl rolled out of bed and glared. "Goddamnit. I'm coming! Don't knock the fuckin' thing down!"

He opened the door and cursed. "Damnit, Carl, I just got rid of your ass two hours ago. Why don't you go home and sleep. I ain't got your money."

Carl pushed his way into the room. His shoulders slumped as though carrying a heavy weight. Something about his mood brought a warning to Earl, and the hot words on his tongue were not spoken. "What is it, man?" he asked.

"I told you before I left here this morning, Earl, I felt like something had happened." His words shocked Earl, and he listened in silence. "It was on the radio this morning, man, names and everything."

Earl walked over to the radio and flipped the switch. Loud soul music filled the room. He turned the sound down slightly. "You heard from Duke, man?"

For an answer, Carl shook his head. "Yeah, man, but he don't know nothing. He says he been sitting in the car all night waiting for Billy to come back. He just happened to turn on the radio and heard the news this morning."

Earl shook his head. "This wipes me out, Carl. I'm busted, completely."

"Well, at least you're still living, Earl. It's all over for Billy. All you have to do is keep on steppin' and you'll break the ice sooner or later."

Earl laughed harshly. "I guess you got something there. Billy sure ain't got no comeback, if he's really dead." Earl rubbed his chin thoughtfully. "I can say I shouldn't complain because I'm still living, but, baby, if you only knew how feeble."

The radio began to blare out the news, so Earl fell silent. A fire on the west side of town had taken the lives of six kids while the mother was next door visiting a sick, elderly woman. Three new gangland killings had been discovered, and Earl and Carl listened without understanding. Mike Nelson, a notorious gangster from New York, had been found murdered with two companions in an uptown motel. Pistols with silencers on them had been found on the murdered men, and the police believed these had been used in the vicious killing of two white men and one Negro male sometime earlier this morning. The announcer continued with some speculation as to why the killings had occurred but finished by stating the police believed it was a drug-related case because of the black male, who was well known to the narcotics department as a big supplier of drugs in the city.

The following days passed slowly for Earl. He was so disgusted that he refused to pick up the small amount of money Brenda had promised him when she got paid. He didn't even stop in the restaurant. She called him on the phone, but he only hung up in a drunken rage. His appearance became sloppy as he moved around like a man in a daze. At night, Earl would stagger from one bar to another. People who knew him shook their heads in wonder. Some mornings, after the night spots had closed, Earl would stagger up and down the streets, going to different corn whiskey joints until dawn found him unable to remember where he was. Then someone would take him home. The girls on Twelfth and John-R would gossip about how much he must have loved Vickie. Very few people realized that the loss of his bankroll was what had really turned him around.

Prostitutes standing in dimly lit doorways whispered among themselves nightly as they watched him stagger from cellar bars to alleys, where he would stand and drink wine with the bums and wineheads. Connie cried silently to herself at times when Earl would sturnble past her on the streets, too drunk to recognize her. His Cadillac would stay parked in the same place for days. Connie began to take the car home some mornings and bring it back later in the evening. She removed the car-note book from the glove compartment and discovered he was behind in his payments. She quickly paid his notes up to date.

She also stopped by the hotel and found he hadn't paid his rent in over a month. The manager knew Earl and thought, like everybody else, that the loss of Vickie had just been too much for the young man. Connie paid the back rent and asked for the key. She realized he was so happy to receive the rent money that he would have given her the key to the hotel. He could have padlocked Earl's room for the rent; since he hadn't, she was thankful.

Connie unlocked Earl's room and stepped in. Wine and empty whiskey bottles were scattered around the room. Earl, fully dressed, was lying across the bed. The acid smell of vomit filled her nostrils. She quickly opened a window and struggled with her stomach as she began to clean up the mess. Earl moaned once or twice while she worked, and she glanced worriedly at him. She was more anxious about his health than anything else. She knew what few people dared to whisper: with Billy's death, Earl had blown everything. She had gotten it straight from Carl.

She went to the bathroom and started his shower. After adjusting the water, she returned and, with quiet determination, began trying to get Earl undressed. With the utmost patience, she finally got him down to his shorts and undershirt. She half carried and dragged him to the shower, pushing him under the cold water.

"I'll be damned," Earl cursed, jumping from under the cold water with anger. Connie slipped out of her clothes. She pulled Earl from the wall where he stood cursing and pushed him back under the water. "Stand still, Earl," she yelled. "You goin' get my hair all wet, nigger."

Despite his being drunk, she was having a time holding him under the water. He stopped struggling and swore. "Woman, what the fuck are you doing here? And what's the idea of you coming in here and trying to drown me?" He noticed her trying to keep her head out from under the water, and he pushed it under the strong stream. "At least, bitch, you could have taken my shorts off."

Later the couple sat on the bed and laughed and played. Their mood was gay, as worries were put away and forgotten for the moment. "Well, at least you're starting to look like a man again," Connie stated happily.

Earl smiled at her in return. "You're the bitch who's been stealing my car every morning, ain't you?"

Connie looked surprised. "I didn't know you knew I'd been taking it."

Earl laughed lightly. "Despite what people have been saying, I ain't crazy."

She raised her arms and stretched. Earl was beside her and his words were like a caress. "I made a mistake before, Connie, but I'm asking you from the bottom of my heart: have you come back home?"

The bath towel slipped from her body as she turned and pressed herself against him. "I've never given myself to a man, honey, unless he was mine." Her voice dropped to a whisper. "You taught me that, Earl, don't you remember?" With these words, she melted into his arms.

Evening came and went. Now night had silently moved in. The couple began to stir on the bed restlessly. "It's been like a honeymoon, baby," Connie whispered. Her eyes sparkled with the awareness of knowing that she had been well loved. She seemed to drift when she left the bed. She removed one of the few remaining suits of Earl's from the closet. She walked to the dresser and got a spotless white shirt. "I want you to look good tonight, daddy. I want them whores to see what a real pimp looks like."

"I ain't been wearing my suits, Connie, 'cause my jewelry is in the pawnshop. I feel undressed with a suit on and no diamonds."

Connie laughed and opened her pocketbook. She removed his ring and watch. "I didn't have enough to get your stickpin, daddy, but it won't take long."

Donald Goines

Earl stared at her without speaking. He took her into his arms. "You sure-nuff got the love I need, woman. You can't even stand to see me hurt myself." He hugged her tightly.

When he got dressed, he slipped his jewelry on and turned for her approval. "Oh, baby," she murmured, "you're the only real pimp in this town, daddy, and I hope you never let these whores forget it." They walked out of the hotel together with an air of extravagance. People strolling by stopped and watched the couple enter the Cadillac. Two men watched the big car pull away from the curb. "It's just like I always said," one of the men remarked. "If you take his whores away, a pimp won't even be able to pay his own rent."

"I don't know," the other man replied. "Earl had a bad break, but he still didn't blow his hog."

Earl turned a corner and started down the street of broken dreams. He stopped long enough to let the top down on his car, then continued down the street slowly.

"Hi, Connie!" a girl yelled from a darkened doorway. Connie waved at different girls standing out on the streets, working. "You coming to work tonight, Connie?" a tall, slender girl asked.

"I might come down later on and show you girls how to sell this commodity, if my daddy wants me to," Connie yelled happily.

Earl pulled up in front of a bar and parked between two Cadillacs. Girls stood out in the street in front of the bar. Every time a young Negro male would stop his car, one of the girls would yell: "Pull on up, honey, 'less you spending cash. If not, keep on riding, baby."

"You bitches act like you own the goddamn street," one of the young males yelled back.

"You're blocking the action, fool," one girl yelled as she walked away. "You don't want to do nothing but bullshit, and I ain't got the time. Hey, honey," she called to a passing car with two white men in it. "Turn the corner, sweetie."

Earl and Connie walked into the bar. She clung to his arm possessively. Earl waved to the barmaid. "Give all the gamers a drink, baby, and let them know who they're drinking with."

"Yessir, Mr. Earl, and I know you want a bottle of champagne for you and your lady," the barmaid replied.

Out of Earl's vision, Fay watched Connie and Earl with an unwholesome fascination. The more she watched, the more furious she became. In her alcoholic condition, it was inconceivable for her to imagine Earl picking himself back up. For the past weeks, she had appreciated the spectacle of Earl staggering down the streets drunk. Frequently she had searched the bars just to get a glimpse of him drunk. The sight of him now fully in control again was too much, and she stalked from the bar with death in her heart.

Sister moved up and down the bar, pouring drinks happily. She liked Earl and was glad to see him looking like he used to. She popped another bottle of champagne for the couple. "I don't know what it is, Connie, but it seems like you do something for this man."

Connie laughed. Earl pulled her towards him and kissed her slowly. This was the beginning. He had had his moment of weakness, and from here on out, he would take care of business.

Tomorrow he would stop at the restaurant and talk to Brenda. It shouldn't take too long to turn her out. The quickest way would be to trick her out there. His best bet would be to use the white bellboy, Jack. Give him a hundred dollars to trick with the girl, and he'd do just that. Get somebody else, and they would try giving the girl less than that. He pictured her in his mind. Once she got a hundred for turning a trick, she'd be hooked. He was sure of it.

Connie put her arms around his neck and kissed him passionately. When she opened her eyes, she saw Fay staggering through the tables in their direction. Apprehension gripped her heart. Fay was clutching something tightly in her hand as she came towards them. "Honey!" Connie screamed loudly in his ear.

Earl wheeled around on his stool. The fear in her voice warned him. He saw Fay, and he saw the gun she held in her hand. He jumped away from the bar, scared something might happen to Connie. Instead of moving towards the drunken woman, he had moved sideways, and that split second cost him.

As Fay brought the gun up, Earl dropped his head and charged her. It was his only chance. The explosion was loud, but he never heard it. Her first shot tore the top of his head off. Her second one hit him in the face and he was tossed violently back. The screams of the women never reached him as he fell to the floor.

"Goddamn!" someone cried loudly as the bar patrons gathered around. But Connie was beyond hearing. She sat down on the floor and held Earl's bloody head. It was over, she knew. But it would take quite a while—a trip to a mental hospital and back—before she would be able to accept this night's work.

Donald Goines returns with another
classic street tale . . .

Daddy Cool

Available in September 2014 from
Holloway House Classics!

I

Larry Jackson, better known as "Daddy Cool," stopped on the litter-filled street in the town of Flint, Michigan. His prey, a slim, brown-complexioned man, walked briskly ahead. He was unaware that he was being followed by one of the deadliest killers the earth had ever spawned.

Taking his time, Daddy Cool removed a cigarette pack and lit up a Pall Mall. He wasn't in a hurry. He knew that the frightened man in front of him was as good as dead. Whenever the man glanced back over his shoulder he saw nothing moving on the dark side of the street.

William Billings let out a sigh of relief. He had gotten away with it. Everybody had talked about how relentless the number barons were that he worked for, but after ten years of employment with the numbers men, he had come to the conclusion that it was just another business. Like the well-talked-about Mafia, the black numbers men he worked for depended on their reputations to carry them along. And many of those frightening stories out of the past became so outrageous that separating reality from unreality often was impossible.

Five years ago William had formulated the idea of how to rip off the people he worked for, but it had taken him another five years to get up the nerve to really put his dream to work. It had been easier than he imagined. The money had just been lying there waiting for him to pick it up. Actually, he was the accountant, so every day he was in contact with at least ten thousand dollars in cash. The problem lay with faking out the two elderly women who worked in the storefront with him. William had to hold back a burst of laughter when he went back over the events and how simple it had been. All those years of waiting, being afraid of what might happen if he walked out with the money, had made him ashamed. He could have ripped off the money five years earlier and been in South America by now, with his dream ranch producing money. But out of fear he had waited. Now that he had done it, he realized that all the waiting had been in vain. It had only been his inborn fear that had kept him from being rich.

A young girl in her early teens walked past, her short skirt revealing large, meaty thighs. William did something he never did. He spoke to the young girl as she went past, her hips swaying enticingly.

The girl ignored the older, balding man, keeping her head turned sideways so that she didn't have to look into his leering eyes.

At any other time the flat rejection would have filled William with a feeling of remorse. But now, because of the briefcase he carried, it didn't faze him at all. He even managed to let out a contemptuous laugh. The silly fool, he coldly reflected. If she had only known that I carried enough money in this briefcase to make every dream she ever had come true, she wouldn't have acted so funky. He laughed again, the sound carrying to the young girl as she hurried on her way home. At the sound of William's laughter, she began to walk faster. His laughter seemed to be sinister in the early evening darkness that was quickly falling. The sudden appearance of another man from around a parked car gave the girl a fright, but after another quick glance, she forgot about him. It was obvious that the man wasn't paying any attention to her. She glanced back once at the tall black man, then hurried on her way.

At the sight of the young girl coming down the street, Daddy Cool pulled his short-brimmed hat farther down over his eyes. He didn't want anyone recognizing him at this particular moment.

At the sound of Billings' voice, Daddy Cool relaxed. If William could find anything to laugh about at this stage of the game, it showed that the

man was shaking off the fear that had made him
so cautious earlier in the day. Now it was just the
matter of the right opportunity presenting itself.
Then Daddy Cool would take care of his job and
be on his way home in a matter of moments.

At the thought of home, a slight frown crossed
Larry's face. His wife would be cuddled up in the
bed watching the television at this time of night.
Janet might be anywhere. Without him at home
she would surely run wild, staying out to daybreak before coming home, because she knew
her mother would be sound asleep by the time
she came in. And even if she was awake, there was
nothing to fear because she wouldn't say anything
to her about keeping late hours. All she was interested in was having a cold bottle of beer in her
hand and a good television program. That was
what made her happy.

Larry frowned in the dark as he wondered
about the tricks fate could play on a man. He remembered the first time he had seen his wife. She
had been dancing with a group at a nightclub. How
he had wished he could make her his woman.
Now, twenty years later, after getting the woman
he had dreamed about as a young man, he realized just how foolish he had been. Instead of
choosing a woman for her brains, he had foolishly
chosen one because of the way she was built. The
last fifteen years had been lived regretting his ig-
norance.

Even as he followed this line of thought, he realized that he would have put her out long ago if it hadn't been for his daughter, Janet. Knowing how it was to grow up as a child without any parents, he had sworn to raise any children born to him. Janet had been the only child born out of his marriage. So he had poured out all his love for his only child, giving Janet whatever she thought about having. He had spoiled the girl before she was five years old. Now that she was in her teens, he couldn't remember when either one of them had ever whipped the child. Janet had grown up headstrong and used to having her way. Because of the money Daddy Cool made, it hadn't bothered him. Whatever the child had ever wanted, he had been able to give it to her.

Daddy Cool noticed the man he was following turn the corner and start walking faster. There was no better time than now to make the hit. As long as the man stayed on these back streets it would be perfect. He only had to catch up with the man without arousing his suspicions. Daddy Cool started to lengthen his stride until he was almost running.

William had a definite goal. A longtime friend stayed somewhere in the next block, but over the years he had forgotten just where the house was. In his haste to leave Detroit, he had left his address book on the dining-room table, so it was useless to him now. He slowed down, knowing that he would recognize the house when he saw it. It was on Newal Street, that he was sure of. It shouldn't be too hard to find in the coming darkness.

Like a hunted animal, Billings' nerves were sharpened to a peak. Glancing back over his shoulder, he noticed a tall man coming around the corner. His first reaction was one of alarm. His senses, alert to possible danger, had detected the presence of someone or something in the immediate vicinity. As a shiver of fear ran down his spine, he ridiculed himself for being frightened of his own shadow. There was no need for him to be worried about someone picking up his trail. Not this soon anyway.

Disregarding the warning alarm that went off inside his head, he slowed his pace so that he could see the old shabby houses better. The neighborhood had once been attractive, with the large rambling homes built back in the early twenties. But now, they were crumbling. Most of them needed at least a paint job. Where there had once been rain gutters, there were now only rusted-out pieces of tin, ready to collapse at the first burst of rain.

William cursed under his breath. He wondered if in his early haste he might have made a wrong turn. It was possible. It had been years since he'd been up this way, and it was easy for him to get turned around. He slowed his walk down until he was almost standing still. Idly he listened to the footsteps of the man who had turned down the same street as he did. Unable to control himself, William turned completely around and glanced at the tall, somberly dressed man coming toward him. He let out a sigh as he realized that he had been holding his breath. He noticed that the man coming toward him was middle-aged. Probably some family man, he reasoned, hurrying home from work. He almost laughed out loud as he reflected on what a hired killer would look like. He was sure of one thing, a hit man wouldn't be as old as the man coming toward him. In his mind, William pictured the hit man sent out after him as a wild young man, probably in his early twenties. A man in a hurry to make a name for himself. One who didn't possess too high an intelligence, that being the reason he would have become a professional killer. It didn't take any brains to pull the trigger on a gun, William reasoned. But a smart man would stay away from such an occupation. One mistake and a hit man's life was finished.

Suddenly William decided that he was definitely going the wrong way. He whirled around on his heels swiftly. The tall, light-complexioned man coming near him stopped suddenly. For a brief moment William hesitated, thinking he saw fear on the man's face. The dumb punk-ass bastard, William coldly reflected. If the sorry motherfucker only knew how much cash William had in the briefcase he carried, the poor bastard wouldn't be frightened by William's sudden turn.

"Don't worry, old chap," William said loudly so that the other man wouldn't fear him. "I'm just lost, that's all. These damn streets all look alike at night."

The tall, dark-clothed man had hesitated briefly; now he came forward quickly. He spoke softly. "Yeah, mister, you did give me a fright for just a minute. You know," he continued, as he approached, "you can't trust these dark streets at night. Some of these dope fiends will do anything for a ten-dollar bill."

William laughed lightly, then smiled. He watched the tall man reach back behind his collar. Suddenly the smile froze on his face as the evening moonlight sparkled brightly off the keen-edged knife that was twitching in the man's hand.

Without thinking, William held out his hand. "Wait a minute," he cried out in fear. "If it's money you want, I'll give you all mine." Even in his fright, William tried to hold onto the twenty-five thousand dollars he had in his briefcase. He reached for the wallet in his rear pocket. He never reached it.

With a flash, the tall man dressed in black threw his knife. The motion was so smooth and quick that the knife became only a blur. The knife seemed to turn in the air once or twice, then became imbedded in William's slim chest. It happened so suddenly that William never made a sound. The force of the blow staggered him. He remained on his feet for a brief instant while the knife protruded from his body.

With a quiet groan, William Billings began to fall. The pavement struck him in the back. His eyes were open slightly as he felt more than saw the silent man bending down over him. He tried to open his eyes wider as he felt the knife being withdrawn. Why? he wanted to ask, but the question never formed on his lips. The cold steel against his neck was the last thing he felt on this earth. When the tall, light-complexioned man stood up with the briefcase hanging limp from his left hand, William Billings never heard the quiet words the man spoke.

"You should have never tried to take it, friend," Daddy Cool said as he leaned down and wiped the blood off his favorite dagger. He liked to use the knives whenever he could. They were quieter and less trouble. He glanced back over his shoulder to see if anybody had noticed the silent affair. The streets were still deserted as the cool evening breeze began to blow.

Without another glance, Daddy Cool stepped to the curb and quickly crossed the street. His long strides took him away from the murder scene quickly. He walked briskly but not so much in a hurry as to draw attention. When he reached the corner, he took a backward glance and for the first time noticed a old black woman coming down the steps from the shabby house where the body lay.

At the sight of him peering back at her, she hesitated and stood where she was.

"Damn!" The curse exploded from Daddy Cool's lips as his jaw muscles drew tight. The old bitch had probably been watching the whole thing from her darkened windows. But, Daddy Cool reasoned as he continued on his way, it had been too dark for her to see anything. No matter. He began to move swiftly now toward his car, which was parked two blocks away on another side street.

Daddy Cool turned down the next block and silently cut through somebody's yard. He walked quietly, listening for dogs. His luck held as he made it through the yard and didn't run into any dogs until he started to cut through a yard that he was sure would bring him out near his car. Now his mind was busy. He wondered if the old bitch had called the police before coming out and trying to give aid to a dead man. If she had, they would be setting up lookouts for a man on foot. He couldn't take any more chances.

The large, muscular German police dog jumped up on the fence and barked loudly. Daddy Cool took a quick glance at the house and noticed that it was dark. There was the chance that everybody was sound asleep, but he doubted it. They were more than likely watching television. He started to walk down to the next yard but instantly saw that the yard contained two large mongrel dogs. Without hesitating. Daddy Cool retraced his steps.

Again the large German police dog jumped up against the fence, barking loudly. Suddenly his bark stopped and the dog toppled back on the ground with the handle of the long dagger sticking out of his neck. Daddy Cool took the time to retrieve his knife. He couldn't leave it. It was like a calling card. If the police found his knife they would know that a professional had been at work. Over the past years, he had had to leave his knives on three different occasions. His knives were handmade by him in his own basement, so that there was no way of tracing the knives back to any stores. But the police in three different cities had his knives, waiting for a day when they would be able to tie them with the killer who so boldly used them. For the past ten years certain detectives followed up all knife killings such as the one that had been committed tonight. With patience they slowly waited until one day the killer would make a mistake.

Daddy Cool didn't have the slightest intention of making that mistake. The thought of driving all the way back home with the telltale knife in his possession was a grim thought. If the police should stop him and find the knife, he would be busted. As he crossed the yard silently he removed his handkerchief and wiped the knife clean. Then, seeing that the back steps of the porch were open, he leaned down and tossed the knife and hankie under the house as far as he could.

Without seeming to have stopped, he continued on his silent way, coming out on the sidewalk and quickly walking past two houses to where his black Ford was parked. He tossed the briefcase on the seat beside him and started up the car motor.

Glancing up, he saw the headlights of a car turn down the block, and he quickly cut his motor off

and stretched out on the car seat. As soon as he heard the car pass, he raised up and watched until the headlights disappeared completely before restarting his own car.

He pulled out onto the deserted street and drove silently toward the main street, which would lead eventually to the highway.

Don't miss the first book in the Kenyatta series . . .

Crime Partners

On sale now!

1

Joe Green, better known to his friends and acquaintances as "Jo-Jo," poured the rest of the heroin out of a small piece of tinfoil into the Wild Irish Rose wine bottle top that had been converted into what drug users call a "cooker."

His common-law wife, Tina, watched him closely. "Damn, Jo-Jo, I sure hate the thought of that being the last dope in the house. The last time your slow-ass connect said he would be here in an hour, it was the next day before the motherfucker showed up!"

Shrugging his thin shoulders philosophically, Jo-Jo didn't even glance up at his woman as he replied. "That's one of the few bad points you run into when your connection doesn't use. They don't understand that a drug addict has to have that shit at certain times. It ain't like a drunk;

when Joe Chink says it's time to fix, it's time to fix, with no shit about it."

"Jo-Jo, you don't think the bastard will do us like he did last time, do you?" she asked, her voice changing to a whining, pleading note.

"Goddamn it," Jo-Jo yelled as he patted his pockets, "I ain't got no motherfuckin' matches." He glanced around wildly, his eyes searching in vain for a book of matches on one of the trash-covered end tables.

The house they lived in was a four-room flat. You could enter by either door and stare all the way through the house. The back door led right into the kitchen, which went straight into the dining room, or bedroom, whichever you wanted to call it. The bed came out of the wall, Murphy bed style, and could be put up into the wall after use but never was in this particular house. After the dining room came the front room. Here there had been some sort of effort to gain a partial amount of privacy with a long, filthy bedspread that had been tacked up and stretched across the rooms, separating them. Actually, there were two different bedspreads, each nailed to the ceiling. When a person went between the rooms he parted them in the middle and stepped through, using them the same way you would a sliding door.

"Here, honey," Tina said, holding out a book of matches she had extracted from her purse.

As Jo-Jo leaned over to get the matches his eyes

fell on the roll of money in her purse. "Damn, but that seems like a lot of money," he stated, nodding at her open purse.

"Yeah, I know what you mean. It's all those one-dollar bills we took in. Shit, Jo-Jo, we musta taken in over two hundred dollars in singles alone." She smiled suddenly and the smile made the light-complexioned woman look much younger than her twenty-five years. When she smiled the hard lines around her mouth disappeared. Tall, thin, and gaunt to the extent that she appeared to be undernourished, she still retained a small amount of attractiveness.

On the other hand, when Jo-Jo opened his mouth it took something from him. His teeth were rotten, typical of the person who has used hard narcotics for ten years or better. It was catching up with him. He was as slim as his woman.

"Naw, baby, I don't think we'll have the delay we had the last time. Remember on the last cop we were short on the man's money, so I think he did it more or less to teach us a lesson." As he talked, Jo-Jo tore four matches from the book and struck them. He held the burning matches under the cooker until the matches almost burned his fingers. Then he shook the matches out before casually dropping them on the floor.

"Shit! If you had to do the cleaning up, Jo-Jo, you wouldn't be so quick to throw everything you finish with on the damn floor!"

Jo-Jo laughed sharply as he set the hot cooker down on the edge of the coffee table in front of him. His reddish brown eyes surveyed the cluttered floor. There was such an accumulation of trash that it appeared as if no one had bothered to sweep up in over a month. The short brown-skinned man grinned up at his woman. "It don't look as if you been killin' yourself cleaning up."

"Shit!" she snorted again. "If it wasn't for them nasty-ass friends of yours, the place would be clean."

"I'll sweep up for you, Momma," a young voice called out from the dining room-bedroom.

Before either of the grownups could say no, the six-year-old child appeared, pulling a broom along that was taller than she was. Little Tina was a smaller model of her mother, light-complexioned, with dimples in each cheek. She smiled brightly at her mother and stepfather as she tried to make herself helpful.

The appearance of the child didn't stop Jo-Jo in his preparation of the drugs. He removed a stocking from a small brown paper bag, then an eyedropper that had two needles stuck in the bulb part of the dropper. Jo-Jo removed both the needles, then inserted one of them on the end of the dropper.

"Leave me enough to draw up, Jo-Jo," Tina begged before he had even drawn up a drop.

He smiled up at her encouragingly, "Don't worry, honey, don't I always look out for my baby?"

"You can get right funky, Jo-Jo, when the last of the junk is in sight. You're real cool when there's a lot of the jive, but you get doggish as a mother-fucker when it ain't but a little bit left."

Unknown to the couple, little Tina had moved closer to the table, swinging the broom back and forth vigorously.

Tina opened up the paper bag and removed another dropper from it. "Is that other spike any good?" she asked anxiously.

"How the fuck would I know?" he cursed sharply as he attempted to open up the needle on his dropper. "This motherfucker of mine is stopped up!"

"No wonder," Tina said as she attempted to draw up some water from the dirty glass that Jo-Jo was using.

"Your glass has got so much filth in it, it's a wonder you ain't ruined the dope in the cooker." She glanced over his shoulder at the cooker. "You used that water in the glass, didn't you?"

Jo-Jo shrugged. "It don't make no difference, once I put the fire under it. It killed any germs that might have been in the motherfuckin' water."

"Yeah," she answered worriedly, "you may have killed the so-called germs, but what about all that trash we got to draw up?"

In exasperation Jo-Jo cursed, "I don't know what the fuck you want me to do about it. It's done, ain't nothing else I can do. If you're really that motherfuckin' worried over it, Tina, take your ass out to the kitchen and get some more clean water."

"Shit!" she exclaimed, using her stock phrase. "By the time I got back, you'd be done drawin' up all the dope and shot it."

"Goddamn, woman, you don't trust nobody, do you?"

"Daddy, I'll go get you some more water," Little Tina said as she rushed over to the table in an attempt to be helpful. The tall broom she carried was too much for her to control completely. As she neared the table, dragging the broom, the handle swung down in an arc.

Too late, Jo-Jo threw his hand up as if to ward off a blow. The handle came down and struck the cooker, sending it spinning off the end of the table. The drug in the bottom of it spilled out as the top fell off the end of the table onto the dirty throw rug. Instantly the rug absorbed the drug so that it was impossible for the two addicts to save any of it.

Tina dropped down on her knees beside the table. She picked up the overturned cooker. "It wasn't any cotton in the cooker," she stated in a hurt voice. She turned it around and around, as if she couldn't believe it had happened. Suddenly she started to paw at the rug, rubbing it as she searched for some of the liquid that had escaped.

"Not a fuckin' drop left!" she managed to say. "The goddamn rug was like a fuckin' sponge!"

The little girl backed away from the table. Her

mouth was open as she pleaded, "I didn't mean it, I'm sorry." Tears ran down both her cheeks.

Instantly Jo-Jo exploded as the sound of her voice brought him out of his trance. He snatched the broom from the child's hand and began beating her about the head with it. With one vicious blow, he broke the broom in half across the child's head.

The little girl attempted to cover up, but it didn't do any good. Jo-Jo snatched her hands down from in front of her face and began to beat her in the face with his fists. He rained blow after blow on the child's exposed face until blood ran from her nose and mouth. When Little Tina fell down at his feet, Jo-Jo drew his foot back and began to kick her viciously in the side.

"You little bitch," he screamed in rage. "God damn you, I done told you to stay the fuck out of the way when I'm makin' up." He grew more angry as he cursed and, instead of the sight of the bleeding child at his feet drawing pity, it only aroused his anger.

Suddenly he reached down and snatched the child to her feet. Her feeble cry of pain only enraged him. "You bitch," he swore over and over, "I'm going to fix your little meddling ass once and for all!"

In pure terror, the girl managed to break away. She ran back towards the bedroom and attempted to hide under the bed.

Jo-Jo followed closely behind her. He drew his

heavy leather belt from off his pants and, grabbing the child's leg, he pulled her from under the bed.

Her screams rang out clear and loud as the belt began to fall, slowly at first and then faster. She squirmed and tried to crawl away from the pain that exploded all over her body. Sometimes the fire would explode on her back, then around her tender legs, but what hurt her the most was when it wrapped around her and the metal part of the belt would dig into her stomach and hips.

"Jo-Jo, Jo-Jo, what you trying to do?" Tina screamed, holding the dividing curtains apart. "If you kill that child, it ain't goin' bring the dope back."

It took a moment for her words to penetrate the blind rage that engulfed him. For a few seconds he couldn't see or think right, but as his senses returned and he saw the bloody child lying on the floor, his anger fled and fear shot through him. Why was she lying so still?

"Tina, Little Tina, get your ass up from there and go in the toilet and wash up," he ordered harshly. He waited impatiently for the child to jump up and obey his order. "Get up," he screamed, his voice breaking slightly. He took his foot and kicked her. "I said get up."

"Don't kick my child," the mother yelled as she came closer. "I done warned you about whipping her so hard, Jo-Jo. If we have to take her to the hospital, I ain't takin' no blame for all those marks on her."

"We ain't going to no hospital," Jo-Jo stated coldly. "All this bitch has got to do is get up and go in the bathroom and wash up. Get up, Tina, I ain't mad no more. I'll get some more stuff later on, don't worry about it," he yelled down at her before kneeling beside her. He put his arms under the frail child's neck and legs, lifted her slowly, and then placed her gently on the bed. He didn't know that it was too late for gentleness now.

"She looks like she's turning blue," Tina screamed out. She frantically clutched at the child. "What's wrong with her? Why is she laying so still? Tina, Tina, wake up, girl!"

The mother's fear quickly transferred to the waiting man. Jo-Jo could feel the knot of fear growing in the pit of his stomach. The child couldn't be dead; that he was sure of. He hadn't hit her hard enough for that. No way, he told himself in an attempt to quiet his jumping nerves.

"Oh, Jo-Jo, you got to do something. Man, what's wrong with my little girl? Please, Jo-Jo, do something for her."

If there had been anything he could have done, Jo-Jo would have done it. But he didn't know what to do. All he could do was stare down at the unconscious form and somewhere in the back of his mind he realized what he was too frightened to face. The child was dead. He knew it yet wouldn't face up to the fact.

Little Tina had received her last beating. There

would be no more sleepless nights for the child because she was too hungry to sleep. No more lying awake, hoping her mother would come out of her nod long enough to get up and cook something. There would be no more fears of uncontrolled beatings, beatings that came for nothing. Yes, Little Tina was beyond that—beyond a mother's love that sometimes seemed more like hate.